REVIEWS FOR COYOTE POINTS THE WAY

Those of us who have wandered the fringes of urbanity and sanity wonder how to convey the multitude of small dramas, animals, characters and events that fill our long days and nights, real and imagined. Where people balance the intimacy of proximity with the crisp distinctions of personality. In Kathy Park's fiction and nonfiction pieces, everyone is a novel unto himself or herself. Every yard or mountain or room is a touchstone. Kathy Park opens a gate to each event and character, as if the squeaky hinge, overgrown pathway, ancient trees say what we need to know about those inside their weathered cottage of life. In the white space between each vignette is our own life: a tragedy, a comedy, a journey of epic proportions. Kathy invites us to look at the transmutation of marital annoyance into profound realization of community; the boundary crossing between the living and dying; the fracture of dreams collectively shared. Let coyote point the way.

—Cynthia Green, author of *The Trail Writer's Guide* and *Backpacker's Ultra Food*

Kathy speaks a raw truth that touches the heart and takes the reader into their own intimate experiences of this true life. We know the people, places, landscapes, events or, we long to meet them somewhere on our life path. Maybe in our imagination. Either way, Kathy opens the door.

—Kate Booth, poet, writer, wilderness walker, river runner, play therapist, adventurer.

With a voice as crisp as a winter afternoon in southern Colorado, Kathy Park explores rural life on the fringes and makes it her own. Risk is inherent, whether one is emptying the fireplace ashes or going out for an afternoon trail-ride, and Park's finely-drawn fictional characters, as well as those who appear in her nonfiction, embrace both the resilience and resignation that comes with choosing to live in the borderlands.

—Candelora Versace, author of *Making Peace With the Muse*

Kathy Park
Dreampower Art Works
www.dreampowerartworks.com

Coyote Points
the Way

Coyote Points the Way

BORDERLAND STORIES

AND PLAYS

KATHY PARK

Mercury HeartLink
www.heartlink.com

PREFACE

There are people, dead and alive, who feed my spirit and inspire me to dig beneath the crust, to spelunk for crystals of truth so I can live out the rest of my life—and my death when it comes—with courage and honesty. For example, the women in a federal prison I had the good fortune to work with, and whom I will never forget. Their bullshit detectors have become mine. Their quest for true freedom—the kind that has nothing to do with money or mobility or privilege, and everything to do with dancing on the borderlands of creativity, authenticity and independence—has become mine. I can only hope that every day in some way I remember to set my compass to their humor, compassion and sense of irony.

There are animals that have gazed or burrowed or nickered their way into my heart to remind me about the mystery of simply being alive and present, living each day with clear and pure intention. And every day when I forget, when my heart shrinks and sours with fear or pain, they sweeten it with forgiveness and open me up to the possibility that a different kind of communication on the borderlands between human and animal is right here if I would only listen. For example, with horses, always horses. And once, a coyote that pointed the way.

There are crossroads of time and place that compost in my soul and nourish a sense of community and wonder at the spiraling of seasons, the daily presence of moon and stars, clouds and wind, sheltering mountains and the promise of tender green in fields of brown. Many of these places are literal borderlands on the wild and tattered fringe of civilization, edges that still hold and inspire a raw, untrammeled beauty. For example, the Mojave desert of Eastern California, a high desert of rainbow-hued mountains, wild burros and spiky Joshua Trees, which I wrote about in my memoir, *Seeing Into Stone: A Sculptor's Journey*. And now the San Luis Valley of Southern Colorado, the largest, highest alpine valley in the lower forty-eight, rimmed on the east by the Sangre de Cristos and on the west by the San Juans, the land of frozen, floating sparkles in winter, and of cool sunshine in summer.

My husband and I have lived all but one of the last twenty years here in the valley; last year was the lost year away, and considering the speed and force with which we moved back, we joke that we must have been pulled by a giant magnet buried deep in the valley's heart. To some this valley is a bleak, back-of-beyond agricultural wasteland not worth considering except to swindle its residents of its ancient aquifer in order to quench the bottomless thirst of the Front Range cities. But for others, including my husband and me, this valley is home, not our birthplace but our chosen place, a strange, oft-times hard and trying place, but one that nonetheless cracks our hearts open—a place that echoes with the honking of cranes and geese, where hoar frost coats my horse's eyelashes, where the spring wind scours and the summers are brief but glorious, where the viejos work hard to keep the old Hispano ways, and where the ones that came before all of us prayed and hunted and foraged. This is a place that seems to grow fortitude, resourcefulness, independence *and* interdependence, and most of all, deep appreciation.

This valley also seems to be a place that grows stories. Sometimes, if a storyteller is wise enough to get out of the way, a story can transcend the real events and circumstances that birthed it and take on a life of its own. That is my hope for this compilation: seven short works of fiction, two works of nonfiction and three ten-minute plays, all inspired by the people, animals, times and places that continue to shape my life. Some of the experiences are my own; some are borrowed or conflated, even stolen. All have been changed in service to what I felt each story needed in order to come alive and speak its truth. You may or may not detect loosely woven threads tying them together like echoing colors in a handmade rug. You may or may not recognize yourself or a certain character, town or prison. As for myself, a line from Joni Mitchell's song "Hejira" reminds me of my bearings: "I see something of myself in everyone / just at this moment of the world."

Coyote Points
the Way

Illustrations by the author

FICTION

THE SPRING WIND

The spring wind scoured the valley floor, dismembering limbs from old cottonwoods, their soft and rotten flesh no match for the jet stream let loose upon the valley. It tore alfalfa seeds from freshly-sown fields and sent them rolling and tumbling into the chamisa scrub. The shaggy wild horses turned their backs to hunker down close-eyed while the wind curried their coats, whipped their manes into dreadlocks and sucked their warm breath away.

One spring, the wind was particularly fierce and abrasive. When Maggie took the ash bucket outside one night, the cold wind bit into her bare arms. She never seemed to have the right clothes on with the weather oscillating back and forth between warm and cold like it had bipolar disorder. She didn't want to linger under the cold glitter of stars any more than she had to, but she wasn't ready to go back inside either. She sat down on a bench sheltered from the wind and lit a joint, sucking hungrily at the sweet smoke as if its warmth could stop her shivering. She thought maybe some of the shivers weren't due to the cold, but because she was angry with Paul, again.

She could see the blue glow of the TV through the living room window, and if she leaned forward a little, she could see Paul in the rocking chair, his eyes mirroring the flickering images on the screen. The only time he seemed to come alive was when he picked up the remote and surfed the channels, as he was doing now. The strobing effect of the shifting screen gave her a headache, so she leaned back and tugged on the joint again.

Why hadn't HE thought to empty the ash bucket so they could build a fire? Why wasn't he finding a job? Why did he wait for her to get home from work before he roused himself to fix anything around the house? Why did he stare at screens all day, if not the TV, then the computer, shopping, always shopping for the best deal? And whose money was he spending anyway? She could feel herself contracting inside, some place that used to feel full and expansive and hopeful. Now she felt shriveled, like a tender plant in this desiccating wind, just like the new shoots of spinach in the garden that had been sand-blasted yesterday morning. Despite the wooden fence they'd built to shelter the garden, the wind had also flattened the peas and stripped off the new blossoms from the apple trees, apricot trees, and sole surviving peach tree. She had stood in the shelter of the doorway, shielded her eyes from the coarse wind, and cried.

Maggie remembered a microburst last spring that had peeled up her neighbor Bonnie's roof like a sardine can, toppling the entire structure on her granddaughter's bicycles which they had parked outside the house not twenty minutes before. The wind had sucked the insulation high into the sky and spread it downwind in drifts of fluffy pink snow until it caught in the sage. And two springs ago the wind had ripped off the tin roof of Roberto's hay shed and sent it across the road like a spinning guillotine, severing the power lines and sending them into a wild snake dance of blue sparks.

Maggie sucked on the last of the sweet smoke and stubbed the roach out in the ash bucket. She could see that Paul was still entranced by the TV's blue glow. Sighing, she trudged out into the cold wind to empty the bucket on the ash pile near the workshop. She figured she'd slip inside the house quietly, climb upstairs to the loft, curl up with the cats, listen to the owls hooting in the big blue spruce outside the window, and fall asleep to a good novel. He could build a fire if he wanted to, but she hoped she'd be asleep by the time he came upstairs.

Around two in the morning, Maggie woke with a start, scaring the cats off the bed. Paul snored beside her, but she knew in her gut that something was wrong. She could see moonglow outside, but the color seemed off, pinker than it should be. Then she smelled smoke.

"Paul, get up! Something's on fire!" she yelled as she dove into her clothes and raced down the ladder.

"Hunh?" Paul mumbled.

"Get your ass out of bed! NOW!"

As she raced out the door she could hear Paul stamping about upstairs. The wind had eased only a little but the cold still penetrated through the jacket she'd thrown on. When she rounded the corner of the house she gasped. Orange flames licked and writhed up the wall of the workshop, sparks flew to the stars, and smoke obscured the waxing moon.

"Call 911!" she yelled back into the house at Paul as she raced for the garden hose coiled by the well-house out by the garden. The hose felt stiff with cold and she suddenly dreaded the moment when she'd lift the handle of the pump. The water would be frozen; she knew it. *Damn you Paul, you never drain the hose. You lazy bum.*

Her fingers fumbled as she tried to screw the hose on. She couldn't get the threads lined up right. *To hell with it. I don't care if it leaks. Just get water on that fire!* She lifted the pump handle as far as it would go and felt her breath catch. *No sound. Damn it!* She grabbed the hose, wringing it, bending it, twisting it, until finally she heard a small crackling inside, the ice breaking up and the water moving in a meager flow. *Maybe it would be enough.* She raced to the fire with the other end of the hose and jetted what water there was onto the flames by squeezing the hose end with her thumb. She could see Paul racing in and out of the house with buckets, hear him yelling that the firemen were coming. When one thumb got sore, Maggie switched to the other, although her right thumb was much more adept at directing the flames. Even so, she saw without a doubt that the wind-driven flames were no match for her spray or Paul's frantic buckets. Despite their efforts, the fire danced and thrived.

Within half an hour, a big fire truck lumbered up the driveway with a few pickups on its tail. She'd seen their headlights coming fast from afar. She wasn't surprised to realize that the fire had roused at least some neighbors from their sleep. Some would slumber on, but in a small town like this, most would wake and offer their help, as she and Paul had done a few years earlier when a neighbor's chimney fire nearly consumed their house.

When the fire truck pulled up next to the workshop, she saw big Miguel and his brothers-in-law, the town's volunteer firemen, hustle to hitch up the fire hose and turn on the truck's pump, but the amount of water coming out of the hose was almost as meager as her own spray. She could hear the brothers cursing under their breath, muttering about budget cuts and shoddy equipment, and then one of them got on the truck radio to call in the pump truck all the way from San Luis while Miguel raced away in one of the pickups. She could do nothing but continue spraying her meager spray into the bright flames. At least she wasn't cold anymore, although the wind still bit at her back.

Now the sheriff was here with his lights strobing and she had to look down at the ground to ward off another headache. The world had shrunk into the cold hose in her hand, the thick and cloying smell of smoke, people moving about and yelling on her periphery, and most of all, the suffo-cating knowledge that everything in the workshop—all her pottery and mosaics and terra cotta sculptures—was being consumed, fired again.

As if to vex the firefighters' effort, the wind suddenly shifted, sending flames and sparks from the workshop up into the tall blue spruce at the side of the house. Everyone moved in a blur, shifting the big fire hose to soak the old tree and the house wall so the fire wouldn't catch. In the middle of the confusion, Maggie heard a loud motor approaching. She shielded her eyes from the sheriff's strobing lights to see a front end loader rumbling down the long driveway with a big man in the seat. It had to be Miguel. She started to wonder why he'd brought the big machine here when all of a sudden she heard a frantic meow.

"The cats! My cats! They're still in the house!" She dropped the garden hose and ran for the front door.

The sheriff intercepted her with a rough grab on her arm. "No ma'am, I can't have you going in there."

"You don't understand. My cats are up in there! I've got to get them out!" Maggie pleaded, but his grip was too strong for her, and she let herself be led to the squad car.

"Stay right here, we'll get them out," the sheriff ordered.

She nodded, tears freezing to her cheeks now that she was away from the heat of the fire. Trucks were backing up and beeping, and dark figures raced back and forth backlit by orange and scarlet and acid-yellow. Even the wind seemed confused, swirling, sending sparks up into the night sky like a flock of tiny golden birds swarming. She thought of the owls long scared from their roost in the spark-filled spruce. She could see that the roof of the house nearest the workshop was already scorched black and smoking. Then she saw Paul run inside the front door.

"Paul!" she pointed. The sheriff turned and ran in after him, and then both of them were gone inside the smoking house. She shivered with more than cold. Another gust in the right direction would ignite the tree and the house; even a gentle breeze would coax those embers into flame.

That's when Miguel charged the burning workshop with his front end loader. She turned to stare at him atop the roaring mechanical beast. With blade lowered and engine whining, he scooped up the nearest corner of the workshop and pushed it over. Backing up in a hurry, he lowered the blade into the ground even more and charged the fire again, this time burying what he'd knocked down with dirt and gravel from the driveway. Without any heed for the dire consequences of driving a diesel engine into a conflagration, Miguel kept charging until he had buried the building in a pile of smoking debris.

Behind her, Maggie heard a soft sound. She turned, and there was Paul and the sheriff, each cradling a large cat. She took both cats into her arms, grateful for their warmth and soothed by the motor of their purring, the way they twined their tails together, and the way Paul slid his hand down her back and whispered into her hair, "We're all safe, my love, that's the most important thing."

It was then that the fire truck from San Luis roared down the driveway and took over, its belly full of water and its hoses charged, first dousing the blue spruce and side of the house, and then drowning where the workshop had once stood.

As Maggie stood watching with an armful of cats, she thought about how the pestle of wind grinds everything together in the mortar of the valley—sand and seed, blossoms and feathers, pony fur and pink insulation, hopes and plans, ash and regrets—and how the wind lifts this fine grit into the air, rattling windows, pitting windshields, invading houses, and how the grit-filled wind blasts clear across the valley to the wall of the Sangre de Cristos where it rains down on the ever-shifting mountain of the Great Sand Dunes.

She thought about the extreme measures it sometimes takes to feel the support of community, how everyone, eventually, experiences both sides of that equation, the giving of help and the receiving of it.

She thought ruefully about the ash bucket and the joint she had stubbed in it, how the wind must have found it and caressed it into life, and how too easily she let the wind of certain thoughts fuel her anger at Paul.

And last, just as the wind died down and the world finally stilled, she thought of her pottery and clay sculptures, now re-fired and shattered and buried, and how they might look in the morning light, and whether she could make of them a new mosaic.

THE MIRROR JINX

None of us could pinpoint the day the mirrors changed.

Marcello, the town's harpist, thought it was after his long-lashed, pubescent daughter, Sonia, came back to be home-schooled, strutting around his old adobe in knee-high patent leather boots, smacking her gum and setting her black cap on her strawberry curls just so.

Cindy Lou, the postmistress, was sure it was just before Sonia's return, when the old hermit woman with a face like dried fruit said *to hell with town* and moved to its edge with her menagerie: fifteen goats, an ancient Doberman, a blue-eyed pinto that always slipped underneath the electric fence to raid my garden, and a ram with testicles nearly dragging on the ground.

Duane, the ditch-rider, said the mirrors didn't change until after he spotted a herd of mustangs up on Wild Horse Mesa before dawn. Focusing his binoculars on the roman-nosed stallion silhouetted by the setting moon, he had to rub his eyes to make sure he was seeing right: a woman reclining on the stallion's back, spine welded to spine, her long black hair spliced into the flag of his tail, his dreadlocked mane tickling her pubic hairs, the moonlit landscape of their bodies an echo of the mountains beyond.

Still dreamy-eyed, Duane—all 300 pounds of him—recounted his vision to my husband Edward in the post office while Cindy Lou sorted mail and pretended not to hear. Edward told me Duane's story reminded him of a dream he'd had about a tall, big-breasted woman with long hair and creamy skin that peeked through a blue silk nightgown. She'd taken him by the hands and arched into a backbend and then they were flying through the night, skimming above the chamisa and sage, zooming up over the cottonwoods along Costilla Creek and up into the Sangre de Cristos, the pockets of cold air from the canyons tightening his skin and hardening her nipples through the silk.

I frowned, not at Edward's erotic dream because lord knows I was used to them by then and knew them to be a good sign, but because that same ample woman had just painted herself onto one of my canvases at school, only she had three arms, four legs and two faces. Right after the woman emerged from my brush in flower colors—hollyhock purple, calendula orange, bachelor button blue, and penstemon scarlet—I'd gone to the women's bathroom to make sure I'd wiped all the paint off my face. But when I looked in the mirror, my reflection looked smudged. Since I'm so nearsighted I see like an impressionist painter most of the time anyway, I didn't think much of it until I went to the towel dispenser and saw myself moving in a steady blur, not just in one mirror, but the whole bank of them. I couldn't see the features of my face no matter which mirror I tried. I could see my hands clearly, and my sneakered foot when I set it up on the sink, but when I checked the mirror again, my face appeared to be smeared.

It took about two weeks—well after my Kali painting, and Edward's blue silk dream, and the arrival of the prune-faced hermit woman and her menagerie, and Duane's vision of Lady Godiva, and Sonia's go-go-booted return—before everyone in town disclosed the fact that none of our mirrors were working right. Not our bathroom mirrors, full-length mirrors, wardrobe mirrors, rearview or side mirrors, compact mirrors, not even Julie's silver-backed hairdressing mirror given to her by her dying mother. Try as we might, none of our towns' sixty souls could see the distinct features of our faces. We could see our go-to-town clothes and clean shoes, our wedding rings, and the penumbra of our curled, pony-tailed, or slicked-back hair. We could wave goodbye to our families in the rearview mirror, and we could see the coyotes running across the dirt road in back of us, and later, on the paved highway, we could even make out the Texas plates on the SUV's about to pass. Just nobody's faces.

Edward figured out how to shave by the feel of it, and when he wasn't sure he'd gotten all the stubble, he asked me to test by rubbing his cheek against mine. I'd purr if he felt like 600 grit sandpaper and growl if he felt like 60. But most of the farmers said to hell with shaving without a mirror and grew raggedy beards, which made their wives wince, stay up later and get up even earlier. One enterprising young man turned a corner of his woodshop into a barbershop, and

Duane said he'd be the first customer. Maybe he wanted to look his best in case he ran into Lady Godiva again.

For myself, I was thrilled with the demise of the mirrors. Even on a good day, mirrors feel like liars, cheats, and thieves. The way they exaggerate asymmetry so I mistake myself for one of Picasso's women. The way they twist around right and left, and trade back two dimensions when offered in all sincerity the honest roundness of three. I was much happier determining my well-being by how I *felt*, not by how I *looked*. And if I really needed to know what I looked like, I had only to gaze into Edward's eyes.

I had no trouble convincing Edward to take down the bathroom mirror and the big one hanging over my chest of drawers so I could smash them both into silvery slivers and stick them into wet stucco over the front door to catch the first light in a sunburst mosaic. I filed the smaller pieces round and smooth, and embroidered them into a dress so when I danced by candlelight, they glittered like a thousand tiny moons.

And the old hermit woman with her fruit leather face, her goats and Doberman, pony and ram? She must have smashed her mirrors a long time ago.

The Notary, the Wolf
and the Tattoo Lady

Chloe suspected she wasn't the notary type. More often than not when she notarized something, she was dressed in blue jeans and her fingernails were at least as dirty as the farmer's sitting across from her.

On the rare occasion when *she* needed something notarized, the notaries she used in the valley's central town were more the bank teller type, decidedly female with push-up bras, sleek clothes, and un-calloused hands tipped with glossy pink claws. Since none of them knew her personally, they asked for her driver's license which they recorded with small, precise handwriting in their leather-bound ledgers—proper procedure no doubt, but one Chloe hadn't always followed.

She never charged the fee she was entitled to, even though on occasion her neighbors insisted on pressing a few bills into her hand. She never went to a convention of notaries or even a notary training. Chloe was a mail-order notary, invisible to the state except for her flamboyant signature and the stamp she embossed on the documents that came before her. The fee she paid to renew her commission was incidental; she figured that in a town way out here in the valley's scrubland, a town that boasted only a post office, being a notary was one way she could serve her community.

Her coffee-stained ledger told a certain story of the comings and goings of the little town. It didn't tell of births and deaths, marriages and divorces, ruinous hailstorms and the precise date the town was last snowed in—for that history, you'd have to ask the postmaster. Yet even in its record of quit-claim deeds, pasture agreements, powers of attorney, affidavits, and an occasional last will and testament, Chloe's ledger hinted at the ebbs and flows of farming, town politics, and the challenge of survival out here on the edge.

Although most notarizations occurred in her living room, on occasion she was summoned to make a house call. One of the first happened in an old farmhouse in the next town, a town powdered with red pumice—the pulverized ejecta from an ancient volcano nearby. The cold spring wind clawed the ground and she had to close her eyes against the grit as she walked into the overheated kitchen. The elderly signatory wheezed as he sat tethered to an oxygen tank. His signature on the pasture agreement was thin and spidery, drifting above and below the line, but his handshake was firm and unhesitating. A farmer's grip. No need to ask for *his* driver's license.

One spring, Chloe notarized a flurry of affidavits—nineteen in the course of a week—all addressing the same issue. Two households, both newcomers to rural life, sought to close a short stretch of dirt road running between their properties, a road that led directly to the post office, the truck scales, and a large propane storage tank in back of the grain silo. The same road happened to run in back of Chloe's property, but neither Chloe nor her husband supported closing it. What was obvious to them when they first moved to town—that this short stretch of road was frequented by hay trucks, UPS and FedEx trucks, propane trucks, the ice cream truck, the postal delivery truck, the ditch-rider's pickup, and most of the fifty residents, not to mention the farm kids just tall enough to work the pedals—apparently was not obvious to the newcomers. Even if it *was* obvious, they still insisted that the dust and rumble and all that traffic threatened their comfort and safety. Arguing that there were other routes just as good, they took matters into their own hands by gradually encroaching upon the road with landscaping, parked vehicles, and even a log barricade. Not surprisingly, this raised the ire of many town residents. All nineteen signatories swore to personal knowledge that the road had been in continual public use since at least the 1950s, a solid case for grandfathering if there ever was one. If notaries are allowed to enjoy carrying out the duties of their station, then Chloe secretly relished notarizing those affidavits.

The strangest notary request Chloe ever received came from a woman she knew only as the Tattoo Lady. She'd seen the Tattoo Lady once or twice in the post office where the farmers gathered to lean on the curved counter with its peeling mahogany veneer to talk weather, crops, and the price of beef; and where the newcomers learned The Way It Works Around Here; and where the Prairie People living even further out slipped in to check the bulletin board and the free box for potatoes or a trashy novel.

One morning, Chloe stood next to the Tattoo Lady in the Post Office, both working their combinations on the antique set of brass-framed mail boxes. Chloe snuck a glance at the black, red and blue designs wall-papering every inch of the Tattoo Lady's exposed skin, all except her face. She quickly mumbled "hi" when the Tattoo Lady glanced at her. Instead of the biker babe "howdy" she was expecting, the Tattoo Lady replied with a shy and modest "hello." As Chloe sat on the old bus seat to sort her mail, the Tattoo Lady asked the postmaster if there was a notary in town. Leaning across the counter, he said, "That's who you're looking for settin' right there." Chloe and the Tattoo Lady set up an appointment for later that day.

After the Tattoo Lady left, Chloe waited for the postmaster to offer some tidbit of gossip. If anyone had the pulse of that tiny community, he did. He knew all the old farmer families and local Hispanics, the newer Mexicans (both legal and illegal), and the smattering of artist types like herself. He knew all the Prairie People as well—recluses, city refugees, and sometimes unsavory fugitives escaping the law or alimony or child support. Most bought their land sight unseen, land with no infrastructure other than rough-graded roads gridded out in wind-sculpted swells of sage. Few stayed beyond their first winter. Most came to town for their mail and water. While the postmaster treated them professionally and listened to their sad stories, his wife kept a can of air freshener handy for when they headed out the door. He would let them fill their makeshift water tanks from the well across from his machine shop. Chloe knew him to be a good man with his long sideburns and plowshare of a nose, taking matters into his own hands and cheerfully footing the well's electric bill so the Prairie People could fishtail home in their water-laden and decrepit pickups.

Chloe was still waiting for the scoop on the Tattoo Lady, but either the postmaster had mail to put up or nothing to say. No matter. She knew where the Tattoo Lady lived. In a town this small, everyone knew pretty much everything about everybody else, and Chloe took solace in knowing that her weird habits, being so well known, must have also enjoyed some degree of acceptance. After all, they were all a little strange to live way out here in the borderlands.

She drove to the crumbling pink stucco house along a lane where wild asparagus had gone to seed and the cotton-woods were scorched yellow. Immediately after opening the door to her old Subaru, a very large dog approached. This was no average farm dog, no barking Aussie or Chow mix eager to sniff and say howdy. This dog was tall, long-legged, scruffy-coated, gray, and decidedly wolf-like.

Chloe got out slowly. She'd been dog-bit before and had to work at masking her fear since dogs are so good at sensing it. Hoping to be rescued from her interrogator, she looked to the crumbling old house, but nothing stirred. She hesitantly faced the wolf-dog standing before her. His eyes burned a cold yellow. He made no sound and his tail did not wag; he was all business. She felt compelled to offer the back of her right hand. The wolf-dog assessed it with military thoroughness. She held out her left hand to the same treatment. Then she turned them both over so he could inspect her palms. When the wolf-dog was finished, he shoved his long snout into her crotch. She dared not protest. Satisfied at last with a full accounting of her sex and the olfactory chronicle of her hands, he strode away with an imperious dismissal and proceeded to mark all four tires with a seemingly endless supply of pee.

Just then, the door to the house scraped open and, making no apologies for the wolf-dog, the Tattoo Lady beckoned. Once inside, Chloe waited for her eyes to adjust to the dark. All the curtains were drawn and the house felt cool, but there was something else, a sweet odor, sweet but also rotten.

The Tattoo Lady led her to a table and chair across from a bed set up in what must have been the living room. Chloe removed the ledger, pen and embossing stamp from her cardboard notary box. By then her eyes had adjusted to the dim light and she could see a pale figure prone on a single bed, a sallow-cheeked, rumple-haired, wheezing, closed-eyed man.

"This here's my boyfriend, Juan," the Tattoo Lady said, looking down at the rough pine boards and old braided rug. "He's dying," she said matter-of-factly. She paused before continuing. "We want to get married so I can get his veteran's benefits."

Chloe looked at the pale, bed-ridden man. He was yellow, not the cold acid lemon of the wolf-dog's eyes, but a decaying yellow like over-cooked acorn squash. She looked back at the Tattoo Lady standing across the room, trying to see *her* and not the red, blue and black cartography of her tattoos. Snapping back to the task at hand, Chloe nodded as if she understood, as if her experience were so vast and varied that all this was old hat.

"What is it," Chloe mumbled, clearing her throat of phlegm. "What is it exactly that you want me to notarize?"

"This here." The Tattoo Lady thrust an application for a marriage license on the table in front of her.

Chloe took longer than usual to put her glasses on. She made notes in the ledger and located the place on the document where they would sign and she would notarize. Handing the document to the Tattoo Lady, Chloe watched her talk to Juan on the dimly lit bed. Did he understand what the Tattoo Lady was saying? Could he even read the paper she held in front of him to sign? Could she be sure he was giving a small nod, a flicker of recognition before descending into his wheezing, sallow slumber? The dim room stank of sweet and rotten death, and Chloe's vision blurred.

She suddenly remembered visiting an old friend, his eyes afire, his grip on her wrist fiercely out of proportion to the waste of his cancer-wracked body. His need had lasered through her, made her want to run out into the clean, open prairie so she could breathe again. But she'd made herself stay in the presence of death then, and she resolved to witness it now.

When the Tattoo Lady returned with the questionable document, Chloe hesitated only a moment before she straightened her back, signed with a flourish, gripped the paper between the embosser's jaws and squeezed down hard, leaving the official stamp of her office.

Outside, the wolf-dog let her pass. As she drove up the lane, Chloe smiled a little. Not unlike her contentious neighbors erecting a barricade across a road, or the postmaster sharing water with the Prairie People, or the wolf-dog guarding his pack, or the Tattoo Lady ensuring her financial future, she too had taken matters into her own hands. Living out here on the edge of civilization, you have only to shift your weight slightly to exceed its reach.

ZACK ON THE MOUNTAIN

For a small man, Bailey sure could move fast. While I was still cramming my saddlebags with water bottles and lunch, he had already tied Buck, his high-stepping dun, to the big stock trailer and loaded his heavy saddle into the back of the pickup, all the while scolding his eight-year-old brother Luke to quit dilly dallying and talking to the horses. As usual, Bailey was the boss, even for a pleasure ride on a beautiful Sunday in July.

"Mornin' Gil," he called out. "We got you beat this time. Usually you're the one who's waiting on all of us."

I laughed. He was right. "Looks like we picked a fine day to ride up the mountain," I said. "Who all's coming?"

"Luke. And my dead-beat brother-in-law. Maybe he needs to clear his head from last night. Him and Tracy were hitting the bottle pretty hard, from what I can tell. Matt'll ride Mr. Blue, the new gray. That oughta wake him up. I'm gonna run back to the house to fill up on coffee and then we can load 'em up. Throw your saddle in the pickup."

I nodded. I didn't know Matt all that well because he and his wife Tracy—Bailey's twin sister— were the drinking kind, and my wife and I don't go in for that sort of thing. I studied the horses munching their oats. Next to Buck and Mr. Blue stood Walker, the big bay Bailey's mother Cora used to ride, now the horse I *tried* to ride. In typical form, he was muscling in on the oats. Next to Walker stood the old brown gelding, Zack, the one Cora had bottle-raised. I wondered at seeing Zack. Last Sunday he'd seemed winded halfway through our ride even though we'd been on the flat. But I dismissed the thought. *Bailey's a much more experienced horseman than I am. He knows what he's doing.*

From the north, Ute Mountain swells up from the San Luis Valley like a big round nippled breast. Although the San Juans and the Sangre de Cristos that rim the valley are much larger, there's something compelling about a single large mountain, magnetic in its draw, and I was excited to get a chance to ride to the top. Like San Antonio Mountain, its western companion across the Rio Grande, Ute is an ancient volcano rising 3000 feet from the valley floor, smooth in silhouette and seemingly gentle in grade. Not so. When my wife and I walked partway up a jeep trail, we learned just how rocky and steep that mountain is. But Bailey knew the mountain pathways much better than I did. He told me once that he and Tracy ran up the mountain one night several years back after an argument with their father, Dan. Must have been a helluva argument. When they got to the top, he told me they both prayed, and by the time he got home, he said he couldn't speak for his sister, but at least *he* felt peaceful again.

We parked the big stock trailer by the turnoff to the mountain and got out, surprised to see a shiny new padlock on the gate. When my wife and I first moved here, there wasn't any gate because there wasn't any fence. The road was open and we had free access to the mountain and the petroglyphs down in Costilla Canyon. Of course, that meant that the mountain elk had free access to the alfalfa fields outside of town. My guess is that's why the mountain was cordoned off with a five-strand barbed wire fence. While Luke climbed on the wheel well of the trailer to talk to the horses inside, we three stood with our hands on our hips, eyeing the gate.

"Wasn't locked last week when I came out here to shoot coyotes," Matt said, lighting the fourth cigarette I'd counted so far.

"Well it's sure as hell locked now." Bailey stirred the duty soil with his boot. "We could cut it and come back later to fix it," he added after a pause."There's no livestock out here and the BLM will never know." Then he grinned his up-to-no-good grin. I'd seen it on his face plenty of times.

I fingered a tuft of elk fur caught by a barb in the fence. I was thinking about all the times I'd wished I had the courage to cut this fence. I hated seeing it go up. Even worse, I hated coming up on that dead elk with her legs hopelessly twisted in the wire, and realizing she had been doomed to a slow tortuous death. The memory of all that made me want a drink, so I forced myself back into the present by looking up at the dome of the mountain, feeling the cool morning breeze mix with the growing warmth, listening to the horses stamp in the trailer.

I saw Matt blow smoke circles and then give a slight nod to Bailey. I pushed myself out of my funk. "Let's do it," I said, but my voice cracked a little.

All four horses were feeling good as we mounted up. Buck was prancing and humping his back, a handful even for Bailey. Mr. Blue arched his neck and I hoped Matt had shed his hangover enough to be able to control him. I had my hands full with big Walker, who was tossing his head and ignoring the bit, as usual. As I remembered to turn him in a circle to get his mind on work, I saw that even old Zack was dancing; he looked ten years younger. For being a skinny little kid, Luke seemed to be having no trouble riding him— that kid may have been a little strange, but he sure was good with horses. With a nod from Bailey, we set off toward the mountain at an easy run, following the braided elk paths through the sage and chamisa. Walker settled after a while and I managed to relax into his rhythm as he loped over the swells of the land.

Beyond the stock tank the BLM had set out for the elk, the mountain rises steeply. Pretty soon the horses slowed of their own accord, glad for a chance to blow. We stayed mounted for as long as we could, but when the footing got loose and rocky, and the gnarled branches on the scrub brush threatened to scrape us off our saddles, we kicked our feet free of the stirrups and slid down. Bailey had already torn his shirt and I'd managed to scrape my forearm. *Clumsy as usual.* With Bailey in the lead, we began a slow, labored climb. We would scramble up a short stretch, careful to keep ahead and to the side so the horses' hooves didn't clip our heels, and then we would stand and pant, wiping the sweat off our faces until Bailey struck out again.

Even at this slow pace, it wasn't long before Matt hacked a smoker's cough, and Zack and Luke fell way behind. Gasping and heaving myself, I squinted through the brush below until I could see Luke's yellow shirt and Zack's dark russet coat.

Luke's voice calling up the slope was small and uncertain. "Bailey, Zack says he doesn't want to come. He's getting awful tired." Our horses turned their heads and pricked their ears to catch the sound below. They shifted their feet, trying to find a comfortable way to stand on the steep slope.

"C'mon little man, you know what you gotta do. You gotta to *make* him," Bailey yelled as he removed his baseball cap to slick back his dark hair. "You gotta show him who's boss."

The air was still cool but the sun's heat was starting to penetrate. We waited for Luke's reply.

"OK," he called back, thinly.

When they came into full view, Luke smiled bravely through his flushed cheeks, but Zack was lathered and blowing hard through flared nostrils. Bailey gave them both a quick look over, and then, apparently satisfied, set the brim of his cap and took off climbing for the next resting spot. I watched him go. He and Buck had no trouble staying out in front; Bailey still had his running legs from playing college baseball and Buck was young and muscled. Mr. Blue looked tired but game, but Matt's face was drawn with effort as he hacked, and now he was limping and complaining about a bum knee. Big Walker, although blowing and slick, seemed fine, but with each steep scramble my thighs cramped up. *I'll just have to gut through this.*

When we rested in the horseshoe meadow, I looked back on the valley floor stretching out below. I could just make out the stock trailer and the tinker toy red of Bailey's truck back by the gate. I could hear Luke in the trees below pleading with Zack to keep moving. Squinting at the sun, I guessed it was close to eleven. From this high on the slope, it was impossible to see the mountain's top, so there was no way of knowing how much farther we had to go. We were all trusting that Bailey knew the way.

At that point, I'd known Bailey for several years, watched him go away to college and return a little less provincial and cocksure of himself. But he could still suck the oxygen out of a room when he got puffed up like a banty rooster. I'd had my run-ins with him, mostly about politics, but I still admired him, his grit and independence. From what I'd heard, he'd had a tough go of it growing up. His sister Tracy too. Their split with Dan seemed to get deeper and more spiteful every year, especially after Cora died. It was she who had kept the peace, and loved and ridden the horses, never Dan. But now he couldn't get rid of them, maybe because that would be like letting go of the last part of her. Tracy and Matt and their two kids may have lived in the same town, but a bottle always obstructed the path between them and Dan. As for Bailey, he didn't want anything to do with the farm except for riding the horses every Sunday. With Bailey being the oldest son and presumed heir, that cut the old man to the quick. And the last two summers when Bailey worked in the mountains cutting firewood for the ski resort, well, that cut his old man too, because Bailey had proved it wasn't that he didn't have it in him to work hard; he didn't have it in him to work for his dad.

Dan was strictly an old school farmer. Sun-worn, stooped, thick-skinned, half deaf and all business. Probably a bad heart too, but no way would he go to a doctor, not since Cora's sudden illness and the way the hospital had bungled her care. Bitter didn't even begin to describe him. He was always just making do, always complaining about the weather or the banks or the government, always looking back to the old days, as if they'd been any better then. And now, with Bailey graduated from college and returned, he'd expected so much from him, but Bailey wasn't about to be hobbled into servitude. Not to a field of alfalfa, or a herd of cows, or some bank, not even the legacy of the family farm. Not to anything. From what I could see, what Bailey valued was freedom: the freedom to make it big, or the freedom to throw it all away, it really didn't matter. Dan and Bailey may have lived on the same farm, but they made a religion out of avoiding each other.

It was a little before two in the afternoon when we led the sweating horses through a tangled maze of brush and rocks to a dusty clearing of sorts. We tied them in the scant shade of scrub pines where they coughed and hung their heads, resting their back legs one at a time by cocking them on hoof edge.

I untied my saddlebag and carefully lowered myself to the hard ground. The pain in my thighs had eased up for the moment, but I felt nearly played out. *Better get back into running, you slouch.* I looked around at the rock and scrub and thickets and said to no one in particular, "Not much of a view, huh?"

Matt limped up beside me and grimaced. "Nope, no view at all," he answered as he lit another cigarette. "Kind of closed in up here."

I nodded and sipped from my water bottle. The mountain seemed cramped and hunched up into itself. A cold shiver spidered down my back and I pushed away a familiar feeling of claustrophobia.

Luke looked beat. His cheeks were smudged with dirt, his hair plastered on his forehead, and his dimpled grin vanished behind a grim mask. When he sat beside me, I put my arm around him and drew him close.

"You'll feel better when you've eaten."

He nodded, pulled out his peanut butter sandwich, took a small bite.

Bailey came back from the bushes and joined us. Except for his torn shirt, he didn't look any worse for wear. I offered him my water bottle but he shook his head. I must have looked puzzled because he reminded me that it was a habit he'd learned from his summers in the mountains. Instead of drinking water, he sucked on a round pebble all day.

When we were just about through eating lunch, Bailey stood and stretched his back. "Well, we're not quite at the top, but this is close enough. Wanna go back the way we came? Or go down another way I know, more toward the west side of the mountain?"

Luke's body leaning on mine felt limp and damp. He hardly stirred at his brother's question. My head felt thick with fatigue, a tangle of briars.

"I'm game for another way down," Matt stubbed another cigarette against his boot.

By Bailey's nod I could tell that was the answer he was hoping for. I didn't have the energy to think differently. All I knew was I didn't much like the feel of this mountain, like it didn't want me to be here. It was making me feel twitchy, like I wished I hadn't come. I much preferred our other Sunday rides out into the chamisa and sage, the rolling swells of the prairie where there was space to breathe and drift off into imaginary worlds where I felt strong and confident and powerful. But I couldn't really say any of that without getting the hairy eyeball from Bailey and Matt. So I stuffed it.

As we got up, I passed my trail mix around, and everyone but Bailey took a handful. I stretched my sore legs and looked around at the drooping horses and our little circle: Matt with his bum knee, hung-over and hacking, Bailey overcompensating like small men are prone to do, and little Luke flushed and fragile. My gut told me that even if Bailey wouldn't admit it, we were all beat.

But I stuffed that too. *What do I know?*

My wife has long suspected that Luke has Asperger's or some other kind of autism. She tutors kids who've made a habit of falling through the cracks, and most of them struggle with some kind of learning disability. I don't know enough about it to really say, but I *do* know this kid was strange. Sweet, though. But maybe too sweet for a boy, especially going to a school in a tough town like San Luis. He was what my mother would've called a sensitive, an intuitive, able to get in touch with premonitions and the dear departed, that sort of thing. That was way too woo-woo for me back when my mom was alive, and it still was. But I had seen Luke with animals. He talked to them, and they talked back. I'd seen it with my own eyes.

One of the first Sunday rides I took with Bailey and Luke, I was set to ride Rosie, an old quarter horse mare that later foundered and had to be put down. She was supposedly bombproof once you got on her but prone to kick while you were on the ground. On that day, Luke told Bailey and me that Rosie couldn't go on the ride. Bailey had rolled his eyes at me and started saddling her up anyway, but Luke pleaded with him to stop. Bailey has a soft spot for his strange little brother, maybe because Luke looks just like him and dresses just like him and wants so badly to *be* just like him. So Bailey swung the saddle off, and then Luke pointed to Rosie's belly. When Bailey bent down to look, he kept an eye on Rosie's back leg just in case she decided to kick, and then he signaled me in for a closer look. An ugly abscess had erupted right in front of her udder where the back cinch would've gone.

"How'd you know that Luke?" Bailey asked, straightening. "She wouldn't have let you look down there without kicking the snot out of you."

"I didn't have to look," Luke said. "She told me."

"Okaaaaay...How did she *tell* you?"

Luke stuffed his hands in his pockets. "I heard her in my mind," he said to the ground.

"You heard her in your mind. Riiiiight. Did she speak English? Or was it Spanglish?" Bailey twirled a toothpick in his mouth and rolled his eyes at me again, as if to say, can you believe this kid? But he didn't let Luke stay uncomfortable too long. Grabbing his thin shoulders and tousling his hair, he said, "Sure kid, whatever you say. Let's give old Rosie a break and saddle up big Walker instead. That oughta be fun to see if Gilbert here can handle a *real* horse, huh?"

Luke had grinned hard enough at me for his dimples to show. And old Rosie had rested her head on his shoulder and let out a big sigh.

I may not have much horse sense, but from what I've seen so far, most horses seem to know right where the barn is and try any angle they can think of to head in that direction. And if the barn's too far away, the trailer will do. But after an hour of traversing the mountain's broad and tangled top on that summer day, it seemed that the horses had lost their internal compass. None of them had caught on to the fact that we weren't heading home.

Bailey led us toward the west side of the mountain overlooking San Antonio Mountain and the gash of the Rio Grande Gorge dividing us. While the afternoon view opened up to glory, our footing had gotten much worse.

The trouble began when old Zack refused to move any further no matter how much Luke urged him to go. Maybe Zack was just tired, but I remember thinking at the time that he was simply reflecting our own uncertainty. Of course I didn't say that; back then my self-confidence was held hostage to fear. I reached down to pull on Zack's reins but he planted his feet and laid his ears back. Then Matt hauled on his reins while I dismounted to slap Zack's rump and yell, but his hooves seemed rooted into the rock. Luke slid down off the saddle, a cloud forming on his face as he crouched low to the ground and looked at Zack's distress. We could hear Bailey hollering through the brush, "What's the hold up? Can't you guys get an old horse to move?"

Matt and I exchanged glances. Without any discussion, we teamed up on Zack. Matt began to tug on his reins while I found a stout stick of pine and tapped his dark brown flank to make him go, but Zack ignored both of us. I panicked. I didn't know why then, and I'm still not completely sure now, but hard as it is to admit, the shameful truth is I started beating him, hard enough to eventually draw blood.

I must have checked out for a while, because I don't remember anything until I dropped the blood-stained stick and stared at it in horror. I was dimly aware that Bailey had joined the effort. I remember watching him wrap his lariat around Zack's rump and pull. He got him to stagger forward a few steps, but then the old horse froze again. Next Bailey looped the lariat around Buck's saddle horn and spurred his horse to force Zack to leap forward a few more steps, but it seemed the old horse didn't really care where he was stepping, so Bailey stopped. "No point having him break a leg," he said in Luke's general direction.

Then Zack lay down. He calmly and deliberately lowered his body down on the rocky ground. All four of us stared, stunned.

Luke roused himself to kneel beside Zack. He put his small hand on Zack's sweaty brown neck. His lips were moving, but I couldn't hear him. He must have been talking to Zack, or praying, or whatever it was that kid did with horses. Zack was breathing evenly, but he had a strange look in his eye, like he was seeing from a great distance.

I was startled when Bailey suddenly scolded Luke. "Get away from that damn horse. Sympathy's not what he needs right now. And you're not some horse whisperer!"

Luke flinched a little, but didn't stop. In fact, he put both hands on Zack. He just kept on talking in his quiet way, and Zack kept on breathing easier, lying on his rocky bed.

When Bailey made a move to pull his young brother off Zack, I surprised myself by roughly grabbing his arm. I didn't really decide to grab him; it all happened much faster than that, like my body decided for me. "Leave him alone, for chrissake," my voice cracked. Bailey seemed startled by the sight of my pale hand on his dark, muscled arm, and I think we were both a little shocked at the violence of my grab. I remember feeling really grateful that he didn't react in kind.

"I've never seen a horse just plumb give up," Bailey said quietly once he'd gotten a hold of himself.

Luke mumbled something to Zack, but I couldn't make it out. "What was that, Luke?" I asked.

"He says he needs a long nap," Luke's thin voice sang out like a solitary bird.

We waited a few minutes. Zack didn't get up.

Bailey eyed the lowering sun breaking through the gathering rain clouds. He snapped into action, bending over

Zack to loosen the girth on Luke's small saddle. "We've got to leave him and go on. We don't want to be stuck up here in a lightning storm. Zack'll follow us when he's ready, or find an elk trail. Don't worry, Luke, he'll find his way down."

I knew from the faraway look in Zack's black eyes that it wasn't true.

Suddenly I found myself staggering into the thick undergrowth. I remember making some lame excuse about lunch not going down right as I wiped the hot tears that had escaped and tried my best to squeeze them back inside their prison. When I thought I was out of ear shot from the rest, I fell to the ground. I wished I could stop replaying the scene but I couldn't. Some part of me knew I was just having a delayed reaction, but I kept seeing myself pick up that stout stick from the forest floor. There I am, hefting it in my hand, raising it above my shoulder as I approach Zack, standing there sweaty and resigned. I'm putting my body behind the blow, striking his red-brown flank. No reaction, not even a quiver or an ear flick or a squeal. I'm raising the stick again and bringing it down again, and again, until I see that I've drawn blood and then I'm dropping the stick in disgust. I could see myself standing there in shock, but I don't speak up. When Matt and Bailey continue to force Zack to move, I don't say, "Excuse me, but what the hell are we doing beating an old horse? What's come over us? Have we gone mad?" No, my silence makes me complicit. Just like Matt and Bailey,

I'm still obsessed with getting this damn horse to move. I'm not seeing what's really happening.

Suddenly, my stepfather loomed in my mind, tall, red-haired, hard-eyed and foul-breathed with booze. I didn't want to think about him, but there he is in an endless loop, taking off his belt, carefully turning it so the buckle is in his hand, raising his arm above his shoulder and bringing the leather down while I steel myself against the blow. I won't give him the satisfaction of a reaction. I hide in thickets deep inside myself where he can't reach me, where no one can reach me. My body may be sweating, breath heaving, and heart resigned to the beating, but some essential part of me that he wants to rip out and to steal for himself, it's gone far away, into the precise angle of the broom and dustpan leaning against the wall, up with the dust motes suspended in the air, through a window opening to the limitless azure bowl of sky.

I know exactly where Zack has gone.

Bailey staggered back up the rockslide to where Matt, Luke and I sat waiting, huddled against the sudden chill of a late afternoon storm cloud. No one bothered to hold his horse anymore; they weren't going anywhere. Walker, Mr. Blue and Buck stood where we last gave up pulling them, heads down, backs hunched, drawn up into themselves. Balking must be contagious. Poor Zack must have been lying where we left him, higher up and out of view.

Matt rubbed his bum knee and lit his last cigarette. He may have come off as a drunk and dead-beat, and I admit I didn't like him all that well, but he was the only one of us who thought to bring a cell phone. But the conversation he'd had with Tracy about twenty minutes earlier hadn't gone well. Something she'd said had made his face turn bright red and his neck veins bulge. Luke and I had watched as Bailey marched up the hill to where Matt stood, and snatched the phone out of his hands.

"Sis, now is not the time to be giving Matt hell," Bailey said sharply. "You can do that later. Now listen to me, damn it. Do you remember that old logging road we found on the west side of the mountain that night we ran up here? We're coming down that road. I want you to make yourself a thermos of strong coffee and bring a trailer and drive the back way past Sunshine Valley and around Ute. Meet us by the old gate on the rim road. You know the place I'm talking about? Tracy? *Do* you?"

I listened to the silence, the wind, and the horses breathing and swishing their tails at the flies. I could feel Luke shivering next to me, huddling closer for warmth. I could see Matt grinding his jaw and clenching his fists.

"OK, that's right," Bailey's voice floated down the hill towards us. "I figure it'll take us a couple, three hours to get down there. It'll be close to full dark by then. And bring some water. OK, OK...Damn it, Matt, the phone just cut out." Bailey handed the phone back to Matt who peered at it and shook it and then pocketed it. They scrambled down

to where we sat. Leaving us sitting there with strict instruc-
tions to stay put, Bailey had gone off to scout a good way
down the mountain.

But now Bailey was standing in front of us, chest
heaving, his face a cloud of disappointment. "I tried to scout
a good way down to the logging road," he said between
breaths. "But there isn't one. The rocks are too big and the
scree's too loose. I don't think the horses can make it."

Matt shivered and Luke leaned closer to me.

Bailey looked right at me. "I've made a decision. Gil,
you've got to take Matt and Luke down on foot and meet
Tracy down by that gate I was telling you about. I'll stay here
overnight with the horses and get them down tomorrow."

The three of us sucked in our breaths.

"How will you get them down?" I asked, breaking the
trance.

Bailey pressed his lips together and looked down at his
dusty boots. "I guess I'll have to ferry them back the way we
came. One by one."

"You mean back to the top?"

"Yup."

We looked at him in silence until Luke whispered, "I'll
stay and help you, Bailey. They'll follow me. I know they
will."

Bailey looked down on his little brother. I glimpsed a hint of softness in his dark eyes.

"No, Luke. You're needed at home. Pops will be worried about you and you've already missed evening chores and there's nothing to be done about that. But tomorrow morning, you've got to be there, Luke, because Pops will need your help. I'm counting on you to be brave."

Luke gulped and nodded his head, tears leaking out his eyes. *Eight years old and such a trooper.* I took heart from Luke's courage. Something cloudy in my head cleared, the self-loathing I usually subjected myself to every minute of every day dissipated in the evening breeze. I knew Bailey was right, maybe for the first time during this whole messed-up ride. We had to split forces. Much as I would have liked to stay and help him—and lord knows he'd need it considering how jaded those horses would be by morning with only scant feed and no water—I knew Luke and Matt with his bum knee would need my help getting down off this mountain.

I stood up with a burst of energy. I took everything out of my saddlebag and made an inventory of what we had. I piled up our rain slickers and extra jackets; Bailey would need them for warmth and protection against the night chill, especially if those clouds let loose. Three small water bottles were still partly full but the rest had been emptied. I put two on Bailey's pile and the other in my pocket. I also put the rest of the trail mix, the last of the carrots and the remaining apple on the pile. It's all we had. Matt handed Bailey his cell phone even though it wasn't working. Maybe we were just out of range, maybe there was still some juice in the battery; in any case, Matt must have figured Bailey would need it more than we would.

When the sorting was finished, I turned and looked at Bailey, small, resolute and more humbled than I'd seen him in a long time. I reached out to shake his hand, but whatever opening may have existed was now gone and he kept it brief. He hugged Luke and nodded at Matt, and then we three began our slow scrabble down the mountain.

It was agonizing to look back up the mountain to where Bailey must have been making his sorry camp. Mr. Blue's gray coat reflected the last rays of raking light, so we knew right where they were, standing on the steep, loose scree, with Zack alone somewhere above them in the dark. The clouds rumbled and sprinkled on us for several minutes as the storm swirled around the mountain. Luke was silently weeping and Matt winced with every step, every boulder we had to clamber over. No way would the horses have been able to get down this mess. Despite our predicament, I felt better than I had all day, more clear-headed, as if danger had knocked some sense into me and I could see the easiest way to go. I knew I had to be strong for the three of us.

When we finally hit the rim road and I saw Valerie's straw bale house to the north, every instinct in my body told me to turn towards it. I knew if we could make it to its shelter, I could jog the last five miles home for help. But Matt insisted we stick with the plan, and I had to admit that that made more sense. We drank the last of our water, reasoning it would do us more good inside our bodies than carrying it. Luke placed himself under Matt's armpit like a human crutch so we could make better time.

When it was full dark, I left Luke and Matt walking slowly together so I could scout ahead, relying on starlight as I headed south for the old gate where Tracy was supposed to meet us. *Tracy, goddamn it, you better be there.*

When I saw lights to the south, the way they were bobbing and shifting convinced me they must be headlights. I ran faster down the road toward them. "Tracy!! Tracy!!" I yelled, but I was too far away. I called back to Matt and Luke in the darkness, "She's here! Tracy made it! Keep coming!!" I could hear Matt's faint yip in reply. I took heart and ran faster. As I came up on her rig idling at the gate, I realized the engine was too loud for her to hear me. She didn't know I was there until I was at the door. When she opened it, the cabin lights blinded me for a moment. When my eyes adjusted, I saw her two kids sprawled in back before I saw the half-empty vodka bottle.

Then I spied a jug of water in the foot well beneath the sleeping kids. I grabbed it and guzzled, water spilling down my neck and soaking my shirt.

"Where is everybody?" Tracy fixed me with her watery blue eyes. "Where are the horses? Where's my brother?"

I told her what had happened. Actually, I had to tell her a few times before it sank in. We drove through the gate and after a few tense minutes, we spotted Luke and Matt hobbling down the road. Matt started blubbering as soon as he saw Tracy. Luke too. But Tracy was in no mood to be sympathetic.

"I can't believe it. I can't believe you left my brother up there to deal with this cluster fuck. Should'a never married ya. Worse decision I ever made." She turned her rant on me. "Wha's the matter with you people? Got no sense? Leaving the horses on that shit pile of a mountain and only my brother to deal with 'em?" She caught her breath and launched again. "I'm going up there. I'm going up there tonight. No brother of mine is gonna spend a night by hisself up there all alone on that mountain, not after everything he's been through." Then she broke into sobs so strong they rocked the truck.

Somehow we made it home, but not without listening to our drunken savoir shred Matt and their marriage, and only after I convinced her with my last ounce of patience which direction to drive. We ended up cutting the fence I hated so much, and I wasn't one bit sad that no one promised to repair it the next day.

When I got home that night, my wife greeted me with a hug and a question creasing her brow. "What happened?" she asked gently. I started to give her the blow by blow but she stopped me. "No, I've already heard enough through the grapevine. I want to know what *really* happened."

I took a deep breath. Thank god I've found someone I can't bullshit, someone who understands my history, someone who knows what was stolen from me that I'm trying to get back.

"I had a bad feeling," I began. "I knew something was wrong, but I couldn't figure out what it was, so I told myself I was just making it up and I couldn't say anything." I stopped and melted into her kind eyes. "But it's worse than that," I managed before I broke down and told her the rest.

I spent the rest of the night in fitful sleep full of leg cramps and nightmares and rehearsed calls to Search and Rescue, listening to the thunder and imagining Bailey and the horses weathering a cold thunderstorm with no shelter. Early next morning my wife and I went with Dan and Luke to look for Bailey and the horses, banging our heads on the pickup roof as we jolted cross-country up and down the flanks of Ute Mountain. We'd hoped we would find them lounging by the stock tank, but there was no sign of them, even when we studied the mountainside with hi-power binoculars. Dan brushed off our pleas to call Search and Rescue. Maybe he was too proud. Maybe he wanted to teach his eldest son a lesson. Ever since Dan had driven the pickup through the hole we'd cut in the fence, he'd been glowering. "How come Bailey had to pull another one of his gowldern stunts? What was he thinking? This is one sorry mess after another." But Luke, sitting in the backseat, whispered to me that he knew Bailey and the horses were okay.

Sure enough, by late afternoon, Tracy and Matt found Bailey and the horses picking their way down off the mountain the same way we had scrambled up. Turns out Tracy had convinced Matt to go back out to the mountain that stormy night to search for Bailey. They'd dropped their kids off at a neighbor's and tried driving up the mountain, but after they tore the oil pan out of their old truck and couldn't drive anymore, they'd set off fireworks to let Bailey know he wasn't alone. But that's another story. All I know is the old truck still sits there on the mountain slope, drained of its oil and abandoned.

Bailey told us that he had spent the morning ferrying the reluctant and jaded horses one by one back to the little clearing where we'd stopped for lunch. On the way they had passed Zack. The old gelding had gotten up and moved off a little ways, nibbling on thin grasses. Bailey said he thought that was a good sign that Zack would have the sense and heart to follow, or at least find his way down to water by following the elk paths.

But he didn't.

Five days later, Bailey took the stock trailer to the water tank and set off on foot to find Zack. He told me he had prayed for guidance to find the old horse somewhere on the vast flanks of Ute. And he did. The old horse lay dead, stretched out and peaceful on his rocky bed, mysteriously untouched by any scavengers.

When I heard this news, I felt a spasm grip my heart, but I have to admit that I wasn't that surprised. Luke had already whispered to me that he knew Zack was still napping, and that his mom Cora had come to him smiling in a dream that night, saying not to worry because she'd make sure to send him another good horse to ride.

That day on the mountain tortured me for a long time. I don't know why it took so long to see that some part of me knew all along that it would end badly. I can think back now to all the signs I'd seen but ignored: old Zack tied to the trailer; the memory of the dead elk cow twisted in the barbed wire; the freshly-locked gate; my cramping muscles; Luke's small voice of protest on behalf of Zack; the feeling of being closed-in; Zack's dull and distant eye when he refused to go any farther; the other horses going on strike; and most of all, the blood-stained stick I dropped on the ground. I can see now that all of it was a message trying to come through. What's still hard to answer is why hadn't I listened to it? Why had I surrendered my reins to Bailey? What good is knowing if I don't speak it? Act on it?

These days, when I walk out into the sage and look up on the hump of Ute, I can see the horseshoe shaped meadow where we stopped to rest, where I looked out to the valley floor to see the place I'm standing now. I think about my mother and all her talk about following your intuition and trusting your gut feelings. I think about my stepfather, and my lifelong struggle to get back what he stole from me. I think about Matt and Tracy's many attempts to quit drinking, and my own. I think about Bailey losing a few shiny feathers. I'm glad he moved away because I don't think I'd care to ride with him anytime soon. I think about young Luke and hope he doesn't let anybody shame the goodness and wisdom out of him. But mostly I think of Zack's bones lying bleached and scattered on his rocky bed. Maybe he died a good death in a good place, clean and wild and full of sweet grasses, with no one to bother him. Meanwhile, my saddle gathers dust as I pray that someday, somehow, I'll be sent a horse to take care of so I can make amends.

Coyote Points the Way

Odessa peels off her dripping wet karate *gi* and slips into some jeans to head up the wooded hill, figuring she'll take a long looping hike and circle back in time for supper. She needs to get away, clear her head. This whole karate camp is more her boyfriend's idea than hers. She needs to breathe the clean air of the Oregon woods, get away from the exploded watermelons and the adrenalin-filled moment of facing her sensei with his bow fully drawn. She won't dare say it to his face, but she is convinced her sensei is a maniac.

Magnum Mike. What a ridiculous nickname. And his ridiculous handle bar moustache. Waxed to a fine point, even. What a pit bull with his stocky, muscled body. Lethal and gorgeous at the same time. But still a maniac. She only half believed him when he first told the class that he was ex-Special Forces, now a cop who negotiates with hostage-takers and weirdoes holed up in the backwoods. He doesn't want to just teach the elegant *katas* of Shotokan karate; he wants to show his students real cop stuff, stuff that will test their nerve and open their eyes to the big bad world. Stuff like shooting watermelons with his 357 Magnum loaded with hollow point bullets so they will understand exactly what will happen to the back of someone's head. Stuff like catching arrows he shoots at them from ten yards away. Stuff like pitting her against her boyfriend Daniel, his long legs snaking out to tag her with roundhouse and spinning kicks before she can react or hit him back as she longs to do.

She isn't supposed to take the rest of the afternoon off; she is supposed to be working on her triple kicks. But she needs this hike, so pleasant and cool in the forest. She feels herself settling, coming into her own stride, her own pace, her own rhythm. She pushes her guilt away. *What a relief to get away from other people and their expectations, the pressure to perform.*

Odessa keeps looping to the left, not wanting to rush her return to camp, not trusting she'll be able to keep her balance once she is back with Magnum Mike and his entourage, especially when she sees Daniel's raised eyebrows. She climbs a small hill and sits in the shelter of a twisted old pine for a while, savoring the amber light and allowing herself a small, rare moment of stillness.

But it is over too soon. Rousing herself, she heads in the direction of camp, still gently curving to the left so that the circle of her trail will eat its tail. She practices a few kicks on the way, knowing full well that she'll use them as her alibi. She is sure camp is just over that rise. She listens for distant grunts and *ki-ais*, but no sound comes.

Wait a minute. That's odd. I should be there by now. She circles a little tighter, her breath catching in her chest, her hands running cold. She'd always been so proud of her sense of direction. Her father had made a point of teaching her the cardinal directions, how to set her internal compass. *There, through that stand of pines. It should be there.*

But no. Doubt suddenly seeps in like freezing water in her veins. Odessa spins around, looking hard into the forest. She shakes her hands to shed them of ice. She forces her breath into her belly. But her body seems locked away in cold storage.

A surge of panic shoots up into her mouth. She swallows its raw acidity down. The afternoon shadows are lengthening fast and she has no idea which way to go. North could be anywhere.

Just then, a doe appears followed by another, both heading in what Odessa is sure is the wrong direction. They lift their stick-thin legs high above the brush and set them down carefully, as if the brush were crisscrossed with trip wires. Frozen, she watches them go.

When they are gone, the panic surges up again, hot and acrid. She begins to yell. "DANIEL!" "SENSEI!" She listens to her rising panic as if from outside her body, detached and unemotional like a psychiatrist watching from behind a one-way observation window. *Hmmm, that's interesting. Do you notice that increase in tremor? How long before you think she'll break? Another thirty seconds? Let's set the timer.*

Her screeching is so terrifying she makes herself stop. She makes herself breathe in and out. *Too fast.* She makes herself feel her feet. *Cold and shaky.* She stomps them on the darkening ground. *How curious and comical. The martial artist panicking. Much good all that training is doing her now.*

All of a sudden a golden-eyed coyote ambles by, slowly and deliberately. It looks right at Odessa with calm and penetrating eyes. It walks in exactly the same direction the two deer have gone. It even stops and looks back at her to make sure she is paying attention.

Odessa feels something shift inside like the weight of a tectonic plate coming to rest, and the next thing she knows she is following the coyote. It walks silently ahead of her, looking back over its tawny shoulder now and then to make sure she is following. Part of her still floats above, watching with detached curiosity, but she keeps following the coyote up a small hill. When she reaches the crest, she looks for the coyote but it is gone.

The twilight is now full and deep. She can just make out a dirt road snaking in the valley below and on it she hears a logging truck groan and rumble. When it finally labors into view with its load of dismembered trees, Odessa feels a warm current of relief and laughs out loud. Never before has she been so glad to see a logging truck. Instantly, she knows where the karate camp is, and from what direction north beckons.

STAN, STAN, THE HOLY MAN

He had melanoma. Bad. After the surgery to remove a tumor, it had spread all over his body, as if the knife had released the dammed-up cancer and granted it a VIP visa to spread forth and multiply in every region. By the time we came to visit him, Stan was skeletal, holocaust-al, an extreme ascetic with eyes that burnt with fire. Trish called him Stan, Stan, the Holy Man.

The second thing I noticed when Sadie and I walked into the living room of their single wide was the whale bone, a vertebra polished in places where people had sat upon it, rubbed it and left the oil of their hands. Stan and Trish had found it on a beach near Big Sur, probably the remains of a gray whale, and they had dragged it up through the ice plant dunes and loaded it into the back of their 1968 VW bus, something to take home to Kansas to remind them of the Pacific, of blue infinity and the mysterious deep.

The living room of the single wide was crowded. Trish had moved their bed into the living room so Stan wouldn't feel quite so isolated, and so she could keep a better eye on him. She apologized for being on the phone most of the time to family, friends and art clients calling to hear the latest. Was he eating? Was he lucid? How many morphine patches was he up to or was he still on the drip? What will happen to all the paintings? What about the unfinished commissions? What will she do after he's gone? Will she stay on his parents' farm or move away?

I didn't envy her, helping everyone deal with Stan's approaching death. Dark circles shadowed her eyes, but when she excused herself to answer the phone, her voice sounded even, patient, kind. No, they were done with doctors, chemo, surgery. Yes, his depression was a little better, especially compared to that bad night when he'd asked for the shotgun. No, thanks for the suggestion, but they were done with alternative treatments and strict macrobiotic diets. It seemed that umeboshi plums and brown rice just didn't measure up to pizza and beer, not from Stan's point of view anyway.

Sadie straddled the whalebone while I sat in a straight-backed chair at the end of the bed where Stan dozed. Their bed. The bed they had made love in, cuddled or slept estranged in, spoke softly and told each other their dreams. The bed that was in the living room because... because death was now central to their lives and should by all accounts happen in the living room, center stage. I rubbed my hands together and took hold of Stan's feet, massaging them as gently as possible so as not to wake him from his nap or cause even a glimmer of discomfort, but just give pleasure and help ground him in this impossible journey from vibrant, defiant life to ravaging death.

I remembered first meeting Stan, a fellow student of Morgan, our teacher. At the time, Stan ate a little piece of windowpane acid almost every day. He said he did it to keep his head clear and the paint flowing, and to stay brave. I was living right next door to his studio and late at night I often heard him arguing with his gods and demons, howling with his dingo, only from what I could tell, Stan's howls were filled with much more anguish and confusion than the dog's.

His drawings and paintings were otherworldly, impeccably detailed and dimensional, as if you could crawl into the canvas and hide behind a boulder or bush, merge into a shadow, and later find yourself bright and shiny and renewed, as if you had stepped out of a stale and brittle cocoon to become a creature with new wings, new colors, new songs. At least that's how I see them now. But back then I found his work disturbing; it only served to convince me to stick with realistic portraits and landscapes. At the time I couldn't have allowed myself to imagine what he imagined. It would have shattered me.

Now here he was: Stan but not Stan. Burning with the same hallucinogenic brightness but unable to lift his body off the bed. Slipping in and out of conversations, connection, consciousness. I only hoped my poor attempt to massage his feet would in some small way ease his travails. But mostly I suspected that I was massaging his feet because if I didn't, my hands would betray my own utter discomfort. I'd begin picking at myself, my cuticles, my nails—some small, insignificant self-mutilation in a poor attempt to stay apace with Stan's suffering.

Suddenly the front door of the single wide burst open and a tall, big-bosomed woman strode in with a paper bag full of groceries. You can tell so much from how people enter a room. Does their entrance scarcely cause a ripple, like Sadie, my soft-stepping wife? Do they shuffle and scuff their shoes, tentative and uncertain? Or do they intrude, their heavy shod feet chasing away silence like kittens skittering into the shadows?

Trish, holding her hand over the phone, noted the woman's presence with a frown and whispered to us, "My sister Yvonne," and then, pointing to the phone, retreated into the next room.

Yvonne turned her imperiousness towards us. "That whalebone's not meant to be sat upon like that, you know. It's really more of a conversation piece," she skewered into Sadie without so much as a hello. Sadie quietly shifted to the broke-back couch. "Massage therapy isn't going to help at this point," she knifed at me. Chastened, I finished the move I was doing and let my restless hands slide into my lap. Apparently Yvonne wasn't even interested in finding out who we were, or how we were connected to Stan and Trish. I was too shocked and intimidated to say anything.

Then Yvonne pointed her sharp bowsprit to Stan. "My goodness, you're so thin! What's the matter with Trish? Isn't she feeding you anymore?" She made a big show of unpacking all the groceries from the brown paper bag and opening and closing cabinets and the refrigerator to put everything away. "Doesn't Trish realize that if you don't eat anything you won't get better?"

Then Yvonne marched over to peer at the label of the morphine drip and said something I found absolutely incredible. "Morphine? Good grief, Stan. Doesn't Trish realize that you can get addicted to this stuff?" Stan, who was wide awake by then, rolled his eyes and squirmed as well as he could. Sadie and I exchanged glances, but there was no way we were going to speak up. This was not our house, and we figured that family trumps friends.

It was Stan who handled the situation. Quite deliberately, he pushed the covers down until he exposed his underwear. He groped around for a while until it seemed to me that he was sure he had captured our full attention, especially Yvonne's, and then he slid his hand into the opening in his boxers and pulled his penis out into full view.

"I need to pee," he said.

It was fascinating to watch Yvonne's face freeze with horror, as if she'd just been propositioned by a flasher in a mental ward. Meanwhile, Sadie burst into action, finding the bedpan and placing it within Stan's reach. I handed him the toilet paper, and together we watched, rather reverently as I recall, as Stan peed a meager orange dribble into the bedpan. Yvonne had stood as if mummified up until then, but as soon as Stan was actually peeing, she grabbed her purse and mumbled something about relaying her goodbyes to Trish, and then, nodding in the general direction of Stan, she stumbled out the door a little too fast to keep her balance.

Stan smiled a small, curious smile, and said, "Well, whipping out my dick sure got rid of her, didn't it?"

Sadie and I both chuckled. I went back to massaging Stan's feet, and she went back to sitting on the whalebone, and Trish continued talking patiently on the phone in the other room, and Stan pressed the button on the morphine drip, and the feeling in the room seemed to settle into some kind of normalcy, which seemed a revelation to me—to think that attending someone's death was indeed normal. Then I put Stan's feet on my belly, which Sadie calls a furry Buddha belly, and by rocking my own body forward and back, I could gently rock Stan's body through the whole length of him. I did that for a long while, watching Stan's eyes close and the knots in his face relax and the stiffness in his joints melt while the wind outside danced the winter-bare branches. Sadie dozed, cradled in the whalebone chair, and Trish's voice droned on the phone, and when I felt like I'd rocked Stan enough, I slowly brought it to an end until there was no rocking at all, just the connection of his feet on my belly, and when I let go of even that and sat back in my chair, the air in the living room of the single wide seemed to have a tiny bit more oxygen in it. Stan's eyes opened and he looked at me, level and calm and not burning too bright. "Thanks man," he said. "That was the best sex I've had in a long time."

I didn't know quite what to make of that. I must have looked a little shocked and confused because he smiled that small curious smile again, but this time I saw it was a wicked smile. The kind of smile that could incinerate a lie. A smile of defiant and delicious triumph.

COPPER SEVEN BLUES

From her vantage point lying on her back, Audrey could just see the top of the doctor's head as he busied himself under the sheet. He had sprouts of red, curly hair. At least he had thought to put wool socks on the cold metal stirrups, and the lamp's heat felt good on her thighs, but too bad he hadn't thought to warm up the speculum. Better to go with a woman doctor next time.

"OK, here we go, dilating the speculum. How's that?" he peeked above the sheet.

It pinched, but she said, "OK."

"Can you scoot down just a bit further? That's good, right there."

She looked up at the ceiling. At Planned Parenthood up in Medford, someone had thought to tack a poster of dolphins on the ceiling, but here in the San Rafael clinic there was only scabby-textured ceiling tile—probably asbestos, she grimaced—and a recessed bank of fluorescent lights starting to burn out.

"OK, I see the little wire string now," the doctor muttered. "Just enough to grab. I'll let you know when I'm going to pull."

Oh yeah, the little string. The little prickly string that had pricked Damian on the tip of his...well... prick...the last time they'd made love. A certain kind of poetic justice. She allowed herself a small smirk as she watched the overhead lights flicker. Damian had pulled out in a hurry and scowled at her, as if she'd laid some kind of booby trap, as if this too, like so much else fouling their relationship, were her fault and hers alone. At the time, she hadn't known what was happening except that he'd made a big show of being hurt and angry. She had turned away. All she knew was that their coupling never really worked out and this time was no different. He was too big. She was too small and seldom wet enough. He was too fast. She was too slow. He came easily. She took a long time, and often didn't get there at all. The one time she'd strapped an old electric vibrator to her hand and stimulated herself while he was inside her, it had felt like some enormous, furious bee was trapped between them. She'd come, but there hadn't been any pleasure in it. A mechanical orgasm.

She'd had it with diaphragms. All that sloppy spermicidal gel. The anxiety of putting it in ahead of time, just in case. And condoms? Even worse. Besides, the damn things broke too easily and she'd endured two abortions to prove it.

So, she'd had a copper seven IUD inserted in her womb. Unlike other kinds of birth control, it was promoted as one hundred percent effective. No fuss. No bother. And no surprise side effects like the headaches and breakthrough bleeding she'd had with the pill. She was a little fuzzy on how it got removed and how it worked in the first place, but the doctor had assured her that of all the available IUD's, the copper seven was the way to go. Never mind that no one could explain how it worked. Something about the copper. The important thing was that it *did* work.

That had been early winter of 1976, or was it 1975? It didn't matter. Medford would still be coated with freezing fog, the sun shrouded until 4:15 for a brief teasing glow until it was snuffed out at 4:30, a cold wet blanket covering her life. She and Damian had been in a triangle with Anna. Or was it Sheila? She couldn't keep track of their sexual experiments. Nor did she want to anymore. All she knew was she couldn't let fear govern whom she loved, not anymore. She had packed her VW bug and driven south to live with her sister in San Francisco. But by the following spring, she'd moved back to Oregon to try living with Damian again. When it hadn't worked out, she wasn't that surprised. Now they were broken up for good.

"OK, I'm going to pull on the string. This might hurt a little. Ready?" the doctor asked from under the sheet, breaking her reverie. Shaped like its name, the copper seven was designed to insert like an arrow up through the cervix into the uterus. Once inside, it sprung open so that it would lodge in place. Attached to its end was a little wire string, which, when pulled, straightened the device into an arrow again for easy removal. Or so she thought.

"Ready," she answered, her eyes on the ceiling.

An orange stabbing ripped through her pelvis, as if the screaming sound of chalk on a blackboard were amplified and transformed into sensation. Audrey gasped with surprise. The doctor's head popped above the canopy of the sheet, his pale skin greenish under his mop of red hair.

"Are you OK?" he frowned.

She imagined a nasty comeback, or a snide "Does it LOOK like I'm OK?" but instead she said, "Give me a minute, doc."

When she had left Damian the last time—the morning after the pricking incident—she'd made a decision during the long drive south. About the time she passed Mt. Shasta, still snow-capped and mysterious to the east, she knew she was going to enroll in that therapeutic bodywork school on the hill outside San Rafael, the same school where she'd taken a workshop during the first breakup. She wanted more of what those weird teachers taught. Meditation and yoga and bodywork. Much of it made her feel uncomfortable, but there was also something that felt right. Like preparing fresh clay by kneading it smooth and malleable, her teachers were helping her reshape herself into a fresh pot, a different person. She *needed* to be a different person.

The memory of that decision made her brave as she lay on the table. "OK," she told the doctor. "I'm ready for you to try again."

She felt the tug on the string before the next explosion of orange pain. Inside her clenched eyelids, she watched the searing orange gradually dim to dull maroon and red-violet before it cooled to black.

When she opened her eyes, the doctor was standing beside her. "I think you need a local painkiller," he said, lightly touching her arm.

"No," she answered carefully. "I'd really rather not. If I can't feel what you're doing, I can't help you." She closed her eyes. "I can open myself up, doc. I can help you get this thing out."

When she looked again, the doctor's green eyes seemed puzzled, agitated. His pale forehead wrinkled. "I'm not so sure about this. Wouldn't you rather..."

"No doc, trust me on this one," she interrupted. Then, with surprising urgency, "Let me try again. Let me try. Please, doc."

He hesitated and glanced at the attendant nurse standing by the door. The nurse's thin gray eyebrows arched in a question. They held their gaze for a moment, and then the doctor nodded and ducked back under the sheet.

"I'll tell you when I'm ready," Audrey said softly.

She closed her eyes. She watched the light patterns glimmer and dance inside her eyelids, the colors changing like in a kaleidoscope. Gradually, the patterns softened, melted together, darkened into a uniform screen. Her breathing slowed. She relaxed her hands. She felt the weight of her legs in the stirrups, the texture of the metal through the wool socks, the pressure of the padded examination table on her sacrum. She imagined her womb softening, opening. Softening, opening.

Memories flashed by in a fast-moving collage. She remembered the letter she'd written in the sexuality class when she was in bodywork school. Such a bizarre and shocking class, the women all looking at themselves with speculums and mirrors, all the different shapes and colors of their vulvas, and that bright pool of red inside one woman on her period. Looking into the mirror, she had seen her own vulva, and the tiny opening on her glistening cervix. She had wondered about the copper seven hidden deep within her womb.

She remembered that crazy field trip the class had taken to the porn district of downtown San Francisco. They'd each been given a list of shops to visit—a sexuality scavenger hunt into the grit and grime and sleaze. She and a friend had been assigned a sex-toy store where they were supposed to examine the dildos. They'd been shy to speak to the red-faced, jaded, little man behind the counter, and embarrassed to look at the expanse of rubber and latex and plastic under the glass. Her friend sucked in a deep breath, shook her head and dashed out the door, but Audrey surprised herself by opening her mouth. She never knew she could be so audacious. She engaged the little man in a loud conversation about dildos, natural ones to be had on a farm, like zucchinis or cucumbers picked when they were just the right size. How well they worked when they were greased up with olive oil. As if she'd actually *done* that. The clerk had stared at her and flushed a deeper red. The lone men in the aisles had interrupted their musings and glanced over the bookracks in their direction. Her friend, who had snuck back in, gaped at her, open-mouthed with astonishment. Audrey grinned with happiness. Imagine telling the clerk something he didn't already know, talking to him as if she actually *had* sexual confidence. It had felt great, so liberating.

She remembered that when the class had returned from the field trip, the teacher told them to write a letter to themselves from their genitals. Embarrassment had swept over her again. A letter from *what*? But as soon as she started writing, the words wouldn't stop:

Dear Audrey, It's been a long time since you've wanted to hear from me. A long, long time. Thank God I have this chance to tell you what's being going on. So lonely, so lonely, and so DRY down here. Did you think you could just forget me? Did you think you could just decide not to need me anymore? Did you think if you stopped paying attention to me I would just go away? Well I won't. I live here too. I need you. And you need me. Stop deceiving yourself. You can't just block me off as if I didn't exist. You're not a hermit. You can only be celibate for so long. Don't leave me. Don't leave me.

PS. That copper seven you had inserted a while back? Get it out. There's something wrong with it. Make the appointment today.

And she *had* made the appointment that very day. But what she couldn't have known was that within ten years there would be lawsuits against the copper seven because it led to pelvic inflammatory disease and infertility. And she couldn't have imagined that in that same period of time, she would discover her own infertility.

Audrey's legs were spread wide on the table under the flickering light, the duck-billed speculum levering her open, the doctor grasping the tiny string attached to the copper seven that was upside down and embedded inside her womb. She could *see* it, the little foreign object entrenched in her rich dark folds. She breathed deep into her pelvis and willed it to open. Open and soften like wet clay.

"I'm ready doc."

She felt the tug, the bright pain irradiating her pelvis, the little object lengthening, loosening. When the doctor hesitated, she gasped, "Keep going. Keep going."

He pulled again. She felt it give, slide, a tiny movement that spawned a bright glow of pain spreading down her legs. The trembling of her thighs. Her hands clasped wet and cold. The cool sheet sticking to her belly. Through her eyelids she saw slices of the bright ceiling, the lights flickering and strobing, the little exam room spinning. Her breathing was out of control.

"Keep going," she whispered. "It's almost gone."

NONFICTION

Santo the Samurai Cat,
a children's story

Santo was born in a women's prison surrounded by razor wire fences fourteen feet high. Formerly wild, Santo's mother and all the other cats in the prison had slipped through the fence, one by one, looking for their ears to be scratched and a bowl of food. In no time, the cats were tame.

Mama was as black as a judge's robe. All her kittens were black too, all except one that was cream-colored with black legs, a black nose and a long black tail. Lucy, the prisoner who took care of Mama, named this kitten Santo, but Diablo would have fit just as well.

Lucy would use a napkin to wrap up leftovers from the prison cafeteria where she worked, and then slip the package into the big pockets of her prison-issued khaki pants. On her way back to her unit, Lucy would whistle low by a certain bush, and Mama and her kittens would emerge, mewing and intertwining their tails with anticipation. Lucy would set the food on the ground and stand over them while the cats ate every last crumb. Mama and her kittens liked scrambled eggs best, but they'd eat burnt toast just as eagerly.

One day the Warden looked around his prison and said to the prison Doctor, "How did all these cats get in here? This is a prison, not some animal shelter. They're scratching up the landscaping and probably spraying and making a stink. I want these cats out of here right this minute."

But the Doctor, who loved cats just as much as the prisoners, thought quickly and said, "Pets are good for our overall health, Warden. Medical studies prove that caring for animals reduces stress, the cause of many diseases we treat every day. Pets help reduce anger as well, which might not be a bad idea in a prison. I recommend the cats stay."

"Hmmph," the Warden answered. "Well, all right, but not without some rules and regulations. We can't let this cat population get out of control. No more kittens! I won't stand for it."

The Doctor let a tiny smile play at the corners of her mouth before she said, "Thank you Warden, I'll see about spaying and neutering the cats right away."

When Lucy heard the news through the prison grape-vine, she picked up tiny Santo by the scruff of his neck. "What will happen to you, you little flea ball?" That's when Lucy turned to me. "Kathy, will you take this kitten home with you?"

Henry and I were volunteers who taught the prisoners arts and crafts, meditation and yoga, stress management and creative writing. When we told the women that they were the best students we'd ever had, they joked, "That's because we're a captive audience." Lucy was one of our favorite students.

"I'd be happy to take Santo out of prison," I told Lucy. She looked around to make sure no one was watching, and then she hugged me. Prisoners and volunteers weren't supposed to touch, but we broke that rule whenever we could.

"Thanks so much," she said, her tears shimmering. "I know he'll have a good life with you. Don't worry, I'll explain it to Mama."

When I looked closer at Santo, who was so small he fit in the cup of my hands, I saw scores of tiny fleas jumping off his body. As I carried him through the guardhouse past the scowling guards and outside the razor wire fence, I wondered if the fleas wanted to leave prison too.

As soon as I got home, I gave Santo a bath in the kitchen sink. What a scrawny little thing for such a loud meow! I

was happy to wash some fleas down the drain. As soon as I dried him off with a big towel, Santo gave himself another bath with his long pink tongue.

Henry and I wondered if Santo knew he was a cat because he acted more like a dog. He loved to retrieve anything we tossed, including corks, balls or mouse toys. He'd even jump into the trash to retrieve wadded-up paper.

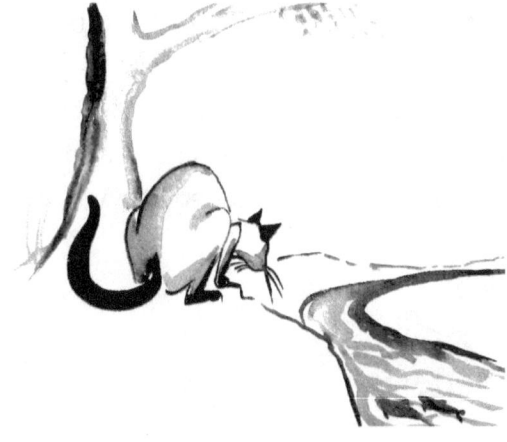

Santo loved to go fishing by the Russian River at the back of our house. His idea of fishing was to climb down the ladder by the riverbank and sit on the bottom step where he could watch the silvery trout resting in a deep pool, keeping their balance in the current with just the flick of a fin. Sometimes Henry and I would join him. We'd hang a sign on our front door that said, "Gone fishin'."

One day we saw Santo cross the busy road in front of our house. Since Henry and I feared he'd be hit by a car, we had to teach him a lesson. I stood by the road and called, "Here, kitty, kitty, kitty," while Henry hid behind the bushes with the garden hose. As soon as Santo came close to the road, Henry sprayed him with water. Santo's dark face twisted with shock as he sprinted back to the house where he sulked all afternoon, licking his wet fur and composing himself. He forgave us by evening, but the hose lesson worked; he never tried to cross the road again.

When Santo slept with us at the foot of the bed, he relaxed his body so completely he felt as heavy as like a bowling ball. That's the first time Henry and I realized that Santo might be a samurai cat, because samurais and other martial artists can make their bodies so heavy, they're un-liftable.

One summer, Henry and I moved to a small town in Colorado. Henry drove a U-Haul loaded with all our stuff and I followed in our VW camper with Santo on my lap. Santo dozed all the way down the length of California, across Arizona and New Mexico and finally up into Colorado. He wore a blue body harness with a leash to make sure that when we stopped to camp at night, we wouldn't lose him.

Santo liked our new home just fine. Although he missed fishing by the Russian River, there were plenty of other things to discover. Like hunting. One day, when we were showing our place to some friends, their little boy, who had run ahead of us, turned and asked, "How come there's a dead rabbit in your bedroom?" There was Santo stretched out on his side like the Lion King, lord of the realm. Next to him sprawled a dead jackrabbit just about his same size. Henry and I scratched our heads. How could Santo be fast enough to catch a rabbit? And how did he manage to drag that rabbit through the cat door?

Santo became a great hunter. Although he never caught another jackrabbit, he caught mice, birds, lizards, and bats. I was sad when he caught birds, but I was mad when he caught bats because he liked to let them loose inside the house. Have you ever tried to catch a flying bat? You either have to net it in mid flight, or wait until it gets tired. That's what Santo did.

When Henry and I would walk out into the sage flats, Santo tried to follow us. Maybe he still thought he was a dog. But I didn't think taking Santo on a walk was such a good idea. Not only were there farm dogs who liked nothing better than to chase a cat, there were coyotes out in the prairie, and great horned owls. So we'd chase Santo back home. He'd sit by our gate and call after us with a mournful meow until we couldn't hear him anymore. And as soon as we came back into town, there he'd be, waiting for us.

Santo showed his samurai spirit whenever a dog tried to visit our house. Santo may have been half their size, but that didn't stop him from taking them on, even friendly dogs. One  day, when a golden retriever came through our open door, Santo leapt on top of him and rode him down the street. The poor, wild-eyed dog yelped and shook Santo off. But Santo leapt on his back again. When he finally let go, Santo's fur was standing straight up and he was so mad, he even hissed at me when I tried to pet him.

 After the traumatic encounter with the dog, Santo had to groom himself with his sandpapery tongue. Then he licked his foreleg until it was wet enough to use like a washrag to clean his head. After he was clean again and his heart rate

had gone down, Santo took a nap on our bed and made his body into an un-liftable bowling ball.

One of Santo's favorite places to sleep was on top of the bedroom closet. He would leap from our bed to the top of the closet door, one of those lightweight accordion doors. He'd balance on top while the door teetered in and out, and then he'd leap to the top shelf of the closet on top of an old quilt. Then, after a nice, long nap, he'd jump down all the way to the floor. Thud! What a way to wake up!

As Santo got older, he began to sleep more, and he was no longer agile enough to leap onto the top shelf of the closet. So he'd sleep on our bed in the strangest position I've ever seen. He tucked his forelegs underneath him so they were facing backwards. Then he stretched his neck out flat. Henry called it the guillotine position. It didn't look very comfortable, but Santo loved it.

Santo also loved our greenhouse. Whenever we watered the plants inside, Santo would meow to let him in. We'd scold him if he tried to scratch in the dirt to find a place to pee, but it was fine if he took a catnap on the cool floor with his back pressed against a sun-warmed rock.

Santo would help us in the garden when we were digging, planting or harvesting our crops. Santo liked our compost pile the best. Sometimes, when we were turning compost, a mouse would scurry for cover. Santo would remember his younger days and catch that mouse fast as forked lightning. He'd chirp with pleasure as he crunched down on some tasty mouse brains.

Santo was never a big beefy cat; he was always on the lean side. But the older Santo got, the thinner he got. We fed him yummy food, like raw hamburger and baked chicken and his favorite, shrimp, but still he got thinner and thinner, until one day, we brought home a young female cat called Patches because her  coat was like a patchwork of orange, brown, black, white and gray. Santo fell in love with Patches. They would sleep curled up together on our bed, a double bowling ball. He seemed to get better for a while, as if he had decided to stick around a while longer because he loved Patches so much.

But then, Santo's body started to fall apart. He was eighteen years old, which meant he was as old as an eighty-eight-year-old man. Almost as old as the vet who took care of him. On the last day of Santo's life, the old vet had to take his hearing aids out to listen to Santo's heart. "It's a miracle this old guy is still alive," he told us. "The valves in his heart aren't working right." When the vet gave Santo his last shot, right into his heart, Henry and I could feel his spirit lift up out of his old boney body.

When we got back home, we wrapped Santo in his favorite blanket and buried him in our flower garden. We planted two chrysanthemum bushes on top of his grave. Now, every late summer when they bloom, we think of Santo the Samurai cat, born in a prison and blessed with a long, happy life. We think of him sleeping peacefully, curled up like a bowling ball and dreaming of Mama, his savior Lucy, crunchy mice, riding dogs bareback, or fishing for big silvery trout in deep quiet pools.

TUERTO THE ONE-EYED HORSE

I have one good eye, and one that stays shut most of the time. Sometimes people look at me like I'm strange, but I like to think I have the kind of face Modigliani would have liked to paint.

Sometimes I wear a black patch over my strong eye to make my lazy eye wake up for a little while. And it does! There it is, blue and shining and open, seeing almost everything my strong eye sees. The words in my favorite book. The painting I'm working on or the sculpture I'm carving. And of course, beautiful horses.

Tuerto was a beautiful horse, but he was also one-eyed, kind of like me. But unlike me, if he had patched his strong eye, he wouldn't have seen anything at all.

Tuerto's good eye was on my weak side and my strong eye was on his blind side. I never learned why Tuerto was one-eyed, but when I first saw him grazing in my neighbor's field, I liked him right away, just like I feel a certain tribal kinship with people who have weird eyes or other unusual physical challenges that prevent them from passing as "normal." But the locals scoffed at Tuerto: "How could anyone want to ride a one-eyed horse? Dog food, that's what he's good for."

Tuerto must have had some Thoroughbred blood in him because he stood almost sixteen hands tall. When I brushed him, I could see glints of red, orange, gold and brown in his shiny hide.

Tuerto's owner let me ride him in the prairie whenever I wanted. He wasn't like any other horse I'd ever ridden because he had to swing his head from side to side so he could use his good eye—his right—to see his way safely through the sage. Even though his body veered a little to the left and then to the right as he followed his head, mostly he stayed true to the path, and I learned to give him free rein.

Tuerto had what's known as a rocking chair canter because it's so easy to sit. He didn't grab for the bit or try to go faster; he was happy to canter through the sage, slow and smooth, so I could relax and enjoy his movement and the landscape rushing by.

My younger sister would have liked to ride Tuerto. He was such a gentleman, he would have stood rock still while she climbed onto the fence to swing her leg over his neck, the only way she can mount a horse on account of her crippled legs. He wouldn't have minded when we tied her crutches onto the saddle. He would have responded well to her "boppers," long leather straps with a ball at the end that she uses instead of her own legs to urge the horse forward. She would have loved his rocking chair canter as she sat astride his big, deep-chested heart. I'm sure she would have quickly figured out to give him his head too.

Since Tuerto and I had such an unusual connection, I asked my neighbor one day if I could buy him, but she didn't warm to the idea, so I didn't press it. I figured I wasn't really set up to have a horse of my own anyway, and being able to ride my neighbor's horse anytime I wanted was already a great deal. But then, about a week later, I was shocked to find out that she had done exactly that. Sold him. The new owners were coming for him that afternoon. Just like that, my riding privileges were finished.

When I said goodbye to Tuerto over the fence, I put my hand on the red-gold silk of his coat and pressed my face against his neck so my neighbor wouldn't see me cry. But then Tuerto moved away from me just enough so he could fix me with his good eye, looking deep inside my soul like horses sometimes do, until I felt rooted and calm and peaceful again.

Not long after Tuerto was trailered away, I ran into my neighbor in the post office. I asked if she'd heard how Tuerto was doing in his new home. She looked at me with her strikingly blue eyes, but that day they seemed glacial and distant, like ice blued with artificial coloring.

"Tuerto's dead," she said, her face expressionless.

I must have looked like my heart stopped beating because she shuffled her feet and glanced nervously from side to side.

"He fell in a ditch and broke his leg so they had to put him down," she added, but it sounded mechanical, like a recorded message.

I still couldn't say anything. All I could do was stare into those frozen eyes and ask a silent question: How could this happen?

But she couldn't, or wouldn't, say anything else.

I had to step outside into the cold wind to wipe angrily at my tears. Why hadn't his new owners walked him around the field to show him the fences and the ditches? Had they let him loose in the dark without giving him a chance to get his bearings? Had there been other horses in the field chasing him like horses do when they're establishing their pecking order?

I couldn't shake the image of Tuerto lying in a ditch, unable to get up. How long had he lain there before he was discovered? Long enough to be hungry and thirsty? Long enough to collapse a lung? Long enough to still be alive when the buzzards found him?

Why hadn't I pressed my neighbor more insistently, shed my ambivalence and named a price for Tuerto that she couldn't refuse? Why wasn't Tuerto in my back yard right now munching on sweet grass hay, his sorrel coat like burnished copper, a smooth-gaited one-eyed horse that was loved by a one-eyed woman?

TEN-MINUTE PLAYS

TWENTY QUESTIONS

Cast of Characters:

MOTHER: in her seventies and recovering
                           from a severe stroke that afflicts
                           her right side and her speech.

DAUGHTER: in her forties and visiting from out
                           of town.

TIME: present

SETTING: A dining room with a large table
                           and two chairs. On the table are
                           a potted rose plant, a newspaper,
                           two coffee cups and a copy of Beryl
                           Markham's *West with the Night*.

AT RISE: MOTHER   and   DAUGHTER
                           sit across from each other.
                           DAUGHTER is reading the paper.
                           MOTHER is staring at her.

DAUGHTER: *(Looking up, pushing the paper away)* More coffee,
    Mom?

MOTHER: (*Shaking her head and pushing her coffee cup away*) No.

DAUGHTER: Can I read you something?

MOTHER: (*Nodding her head*) Yes please.

DAUGHTER: Something from the paper?

MOTHER: (*Grimacing*) No, no.

DAUGHTER: OK, how about this? (*Holds up a book from underneath the paper*) Beryl Markham's <u>West with the Night</u>, Chapter One, "Message from Nungwe. How is it possible to bring order out of memory? I should like to begin at the beginning, patiently, like a weaver at his loom. I should like to say, 'This is the place to start; there can be no other.'" (*MOTHER starts to push back from the table*) Mom, where are you going? Have you got to pee?

MOTHER: No, no. I, I...(*Sits back down heavily*)

DAUGHTER: What is it?

MOTHER: I don't want...

DAUGHTER: You don't want to hear this book? This is good stuff. You'll like it. It's about Africa.

MOTHER: OK.

DAUGHTER: Good. You remember Beryl Markham, don't you? She was that famous aviator in East Africa?

MOTHER: Yes. In Ken, Ken...

DAUGHTER: Kenya, that's it. OK. *(Finding her place in the book)* Here we are. "But there are a hundred places to start for there are a hundred names – Mwanza, Serengeti..."

MOTHER: Ser-en-ge-ti.

DAUGHTER: Right, Serengeti. Good job. That's a really hard word to say. Your speech therapist would be really proud. *(Puts book down)* Didn't you go to the Serengeti when you went to visit Greg when he was stationed in Ethiopia?

MOTHER: Yes. Greg and ...

DAUGHTER: And Laura, when she was a baby, right? Didn't you travel with Jen?

MOTHER: Yes, Jen, Greg and Laura.

DAUGHTER: What year was that? I forget.

MOTHER: *(Shakes her head)* I don't, I don't....'member.

DAUGHTER: I'll have to ask Jen. She'll remember.

MOTHER: Yes, Jen will me-mem-ber.

DAUGHTER: Some R's are tough, Mom. Listen. (*Slowly*) <u>Re-mem-ber.</u>

MOTHER: Re-mem-ber.

DAUGHTER: That's good. Do you want to hear anymore?

MOTHER: No.

DAUGHTER: OK. (*Finishes her coffee*) Shall I go plant this rose I bought you? It's pretty, don't you think? Did you smell it? (*Holds flower close to MOTHER'S nose*)

MOTHER: (*Sniffing, then grimacing*) Yes. Pretty.

DAUGHTER: Do you want to go outside with me and sit in the sun while I plant it?

MOTHER: No. No plant. No plant. (*Pushes rose away with her good hand*) You stay.

DAUGHTER: OK. I can plant it later if you want. Did you want to talk about Africa some more?

MOTHER: No. No more Africa.

DAUGHTER: Did you want to talk about something else?

MOTHER: Yes, but...I can't say

DAUGHTER: Shall we try it in French?

MOTHER: OK.

DAUGHTER: Because it always amazes me that even after the
stroke you can still speak French.

(MOTHER sighs)

DAUGHTER: OK. Here goes. Bonjour.

MOTHER: Bonjour. *Comment ça va ce matin?*

DAUGHTER: Pas mal, merci bien. Et vous?

MOTHER: Comme ci, comme ça. J'ai un peu mal à la tête.

DAUGHTER: You have a headache?

MOTHER: Oui, un peu.

DAUGHTER: Je'en suis desolee. I'm so sorry. Do you want me
to get you an aspirin?

MOTHER: No.

DAUGHTER: Do you want me to work the pressure points on your hand?

MOTHER: Yes please.

(DAUGHTER takes MOTHER'S left hand and massages it. MOTHER relaxes, lets her frown soften a little.)

DAUGHTER: *Ça* va bien?

MOTHER: *(Nodding)* Très bien. Merci beaucoup, ma chérie.

DAUGHTER: De rien. *(Beat while DAUGHTER releases MOTHER'S hand, then DAUGHTER squirms a little)* Well, that's about it on my high school French. Sorry ma. *(Beat)* What shall we talk about now?

MOTHER: <u>You</u> know.

DAUGHTER: <u>I</u> know?

MOTHER: Yes, <u>you</u> know. Come on.

DAUGHTER: Can you at least give me a hint?

MOTHER: No. No hint. You know.

DAUGHTER: Okay, like playing twenty questions, right?

MOTHER: Yes, twenny questions. Yes and no.

DAUGHTER: Right. But what do you want me to ask about?

MOTHER: <u>You</u> know.

(*Long beat while MOTHER and DAUGHTER regard each other*)

DAUGHTER: (*Lets out a big sigh*) Yeah, I know. I'm the one who always talks to you about this stuff, right?

MOTHER: Yes. You. (*Eagerly*) <u>You</u> talk.

DAUGHTER: OK. So, Mom, how are you doing? I mean, how are you <u>really</u> doing?

MOTHER: (*Shakes her head*) No. No good.

DAUGHTER: But you seem just about as good as the last time I visited.

MOTHER: Do I?

DAUGHTER: Yeah Mom. You just have to be patient. It takes a long time to recover from a stroke. You're getting better. Just slowly.

MOTHER: Yes, slowly.

(Pause while DAUGHTER studies MOTHER)

DAUGHTER: But something's still wrong, isn't it?

MOTHER: Yes, something still wong. <u>You</u> say.

DAUGHTER: OK. Let's see. I'll bet that in another five years...

MOTHER: *(Interrupting, emphatically)* No.

DAUGHTER: Not five years? You don't want to talk about five years?

MOTHER: No.

DAUGHTER: OK. How about three years?

MOTHER: <u>No.</u>

DAUGHTER: All right. How about one year?

MOTHER: Maybe. Maybe one year. But, but...

DAUGHTER: What?

MOTHER: You <u>say</u>.

DAUGHTER: But how is it going to happen?

MOTHER: *(Leaning forward)* Yes, yes. How is it going to happen?

DAUGHTER: Well, I don't know. I don't know how it's going to happen. We all have to figure that out.

MOTHER: Yes, but how? You say.

DAUGHTER: Well Mom, I can't say how it's going to happen for you.

MOTHER: *(Agitated)* No, you say. You say how.

DAUGHTER: OK Mom, I'll try. *(Pushes back from the table, stretches a kink in her neck)* Well, I figure we each just know, you know, when it's time. Like Dad. He knew, didn't he?

MOTHER: Yes, Dob knew.

DAUGHTER: No, not Dob. Dave. Rob is downstairs in the garage working on something, isn't he?

MOTHER: Dob downstairs.

DAUGHTER: Almost. Rob is downstairs. But Dad's name was Dave.

MOTHER: Dob doesn't know. *(Shakes her head)* Dob doesn't get it.

DAUGHTER: You mean Rob? Rob doesn't get it?

MOTHER: No. You tell him. You tell Dob.

DAUGHTER: You mean Rob, not Dob. But wait a minute. Weren't we talking about Dad?

MOTHER: Yes, Dad. Dob, Dob...

DAUGHTER: Slow down, Mom. You can get this. Dad's name was Dave.

MOTHER: Dave. Yes, Dave. *(Tearing up)* But how... how did Dave...?

DAUGHTER: How did he know?

MOTHER: Yes, how did he <u>know</u>?

DAUGHTER: I think he just decided. Inside.

MOTHER: Tell me.

DAUGHTER: Tell you the story? Okay. But you tell me if I get it wrong, okay?

MOTHER: Okay.

DAUGHTER: So Dad was in the hospital because he fell and broke his hip. They think it was post polio syndrome, right?

MOTHER: *(With great effort)* Post po-li-o syn-drome.

DAUGHTER: Good. But he came home to recuperate. And one evening you came back into the bedroom to ask if he wanted supper brought to him, and he said...

MOTHER: He said he could walk.

DAUGHTER: Right, and you said, "Dave, you can't walk. Your hip is broken." And he said...

MOTHER: "Yes I can."

DAUGHTER: Right, and you said, "Then show me." And he tried to get up out of bed, but...

MOTHER: He couldn't...he couldn't...oh you say.

DAUGHTER: He couldn't swing his legs over. So he lay back down. And you brought him supper, just like every other evening.

MOTHER: But then...you say.

DAUGHTER: So then later, when you were getting ready to go to bed, you came in to kiss Dad goodnight, and he told you that he loved you and you looked beautiful.

MOTHER: Booful. He said...he said I looked beau-ti-ful.

DAUGHTER: And I bet you were. And he kissed you goodnight, and you went to sleep in the other room so the nurse could look in on him, and then early next morning she woke you up because...because Dad was gone. He died in his sleep.

MOTHER: Yes, he died in his sleep.

DAUGHTER: I think he had had enough and he decided to go. And that's when you called all of us.

MOTHER: Yes, yes. But can I....Can I...

DAUGHTER: Can you decide like Dad did? Yeah. I think maybe sometimes that's how it happens. We get a chance to go inside and decide when it's time. When we've had enough.

MOTHER: Had enough. *(Reaches for DAUGHTER'S hand)* You, you. You help me?

DAUGHTER: Can I help you? Of course, when I'm here, I'll help you as much as I can.

MOTHER: You ask me twenny questions?

DAUGHTER: Sure Mom, I can ask you twenty questions.

MOTHER: You help me. Good. You help me go.

DAUGHTER: *(Suddenly not understanding)* Whoa, wait a minute, Mom, you know I can't actually <u>do</u> it for you. I can't do that. You know that, right Mom?

MOTHER: Dob can't help me. He doesn't get it.

DAUGHTER: I believe you. But Mom, Rob can't help you, not with something like that, and neither can Greg or Jen, or me. Not with this. This is one of the biggest decisions you'll ever make in your...

MOTHER: Go on...you say.

DAUGHTER: This is a decision you have to make all by yourself.

MOTHER: Myself.

DAUGHTER: Yeah, all by yourself.

MOTHER: <u>You</u> help me do it all by myself. You help me <u>do</u> it, all by myself.

<u>END</u>

Something Old, Something Deep

Author's Note: Between 1990 and 1994, I was a volunteer in a federal women's prison. I helped found, administer and teach in the Prison Integrated Health Program, a volunteer-run organization which delivered holistic health to prisoners and staff, the only such program in its day. The scene dramatized here is based on several conflated characters; it presents a true story in its essence, if not in its details. A "shot" is prison slang for the documentation of an infraction or incident. SHU (pronounced "shoe") stands for Security Housing Unit where prisoners are "put in the hole" in solitary confinement for disciplinary or security reasons.

Cast of Characters:

IDA: a young female prisoner dressed in unflattering, prison-issued khaki pants and shirt. She's been sentenced to 20 years and knows all too well how to cop an attitude.

ASSISTANT WARDEN: a stout middle-aged female dressed in a navy blue blazer and skirt with ugly heels, and carrying a clipboard and small notepad. She aspires to be Warden of the prison.

OFFICER EDGEWOOD: a twitchy male guard dressed in uniform. He is sleazy and overblown in nature, prone to aggressive behavior, and has ambitions to increase his rank.

TIME: early 1990s

SETTING: Outdoor walkway in the prison compound. Concertina razor wire in the distance.

AT RISE: ASSISTANT WARDEN and OFFICER EDGEWOOD enter from stage right.

ASSISTANT WARDEN: *(Studying her clipboard)* Officer Edgewood, I see Ida Sanchez is up to three shots for this week already. Have you got your eye on her?

OFFICER EDGEWOOD: Yes ma'am I sure do. That one's a trouble maker if you ask me. Talk about an attitude-copping machine. Whoo-eee, that little spitfire takes the cake!

ASSISTANT WARDEN: Office Edgewood. That's quite enough histrionics, thank you very much.

OFFICER EDGEWOOD: Histri...what?

ASSISTANT WARDEN: Histrionics. Overwrought drama-tizations. Oh never mind. *(To herself)* If I ever get promoted to Warden of this prison, I would never allow such informalities.

(OFFICER EDGEWOOD doesn't quite get it, and makes little effort to disguise his disdain for ASSISTANT WARDEN. Before ASSISTANT WARDEN can respond to OFFICER EDGEWOOD'S insubordination, IDA enters from stage left. The moment IDA sees ASSISTANT WARDEN and OFFICER EDGEWOOD, she immediately cops an attitude in her walk)

OFFICER EDGEWOOD: Okay, little lady, just where do you think you're going?

IDA: *(Still walking)* KP duty. And I'm just minding my own business. Like I always do.

OFFICER EDGEWOOD: Oh yeah? We'll I'm about to mind <u>your</u> business. Hold it right there.

(IDA puts her hands on her hips and attempts to stare down OFFICER EDGEWOOD)

One more smarty pants move out of you and I'll bend you over my knee!

IDA: *(Biting back her temper)* I'd like to see you try it.

OFFICER EDGEWOOD: That's enough lip out of you...

ASSISTANT WARDEN: *(Intervening)* All right, Officer Edgewood, that's enough.

OFFICER EDGEWOOD: But it's my job....

ASSISTANT WARDEN: Yes, and thank you very much. I think I can handle it from here... *(Cutting off OFFICER EDGEWOOD'S protestations)*...and if I can't, I certainly know who to call.

(Huffily, OFFICER EDGEWOOD exits stage right. ASSISTANT WARDEN shakes her head at IDA and begins to write up a shot)

IDA: *(Sotto voce)* Shit.

ASSISTANT WARDEN: What was that?

IDA: Nothing.

ASSISTANT WARDEN: Nothing, what?

IDA: *(Reluctantly)* Nothing, ma'am.

ASSISTANT WARDEN: That's better. *(Looking through her clipboard)* After I finish writing up this shot, you've up to four for the week. Five shots and you're in the SHU the entire weekend. Do I make myself clear?

(Suddenly, as if remembering something, IDA begins to breathe noisily, closes her eyes and puts her hands into a mudra. ASSISTANT WARDEN stops writing up the shot)

What in God's name are you doing?

IDA: Meditating, ma'am.

ASSISTANT WARDEN: Uh huh. *(Looks at IDA suspiciously)* Let me ask you something, Ida. How long have you been incarcerated?

IDA: *(Still meditating)*? Ten years, two months and fourteen days, ma'am.

ASSISTANT WARDEN: And in all that time, why do you suppose it has taken you so long to learn how things work around here? Are you a slow learner or what?

IDA: *(Between breaths, calmly)* Trouble with authority, ma'am.

ASSISTANT WARDEN: *(Sotto voce)* Now that's an under-statement. *(To IDA)* Let me put it this way. Do you actually <u>want</u> to get out of prison?

IDA: With all my heart, ma'am.

ASSISTANT WARDEN: And how much more time have you got?

IDA: At the rate I'm going, at least another ten years.

ASSISTANT WARDEN: Do you think you're ever going to figure out how to turn hard time into easy time?

IDA: (*Breaking out of meditation mode*) Sure, if y'all would just cut me a break. (*catching herself*) Ma'am.

ASSISTANT WARDEN: "Cut me a break." Seems to me that's all I hear around here. I'll cut you a break, young lady, if and when you deserve it. Do you understand?

IDA: Yes ma'am.

ASSISTANT WARDEN: (*Looking at her watch*) Aren't you supposed to be at KP duty?

IDA: No ma'am. They don't need me today. Not 'til tomorrow. Ma'am.

ASSISTANT WARDEN: Is that so? Then why didn't you tell that to Officer Edgewood?

IDA: Who, that peckerwood? (*Catching herself*) Musta gotten confused. Ma'am. (*Begins meditating again*)

ASSISTANT WARDEN: Uh huh. So where are you really headed?

IDA: Back to my unit, ma'am.

ASSISTANT WARDEN: *(Peers at IDA even closer)* What did you say you were doing?

IDA: Meditating, ma'am.

ASSISTANT WARDEN: Meditating. Right here in the middle of the prison compound?

IDA: Yes ma'am.

ASSISTANT WARDEN: *(Sarcastically)* Don't you have your special little stress management group for meditating and whatever else it is that you do?

IDA: Yes ma'am.

ASSISTANT WARDEN: Well then would you mind telling me why the hell you're meditating right here, right now?

IDA: Teacher told me to practice every chance I get, ma'am.

ASSISTANT WARDEN: The teacher told you to.

IDA: Yes ma'am. Anger management, ma'am.

(ASSISTANT WARDEN stares at IDA, who goes back to exaggerated breathing. ASSISTANT WARDEN shakes her head and goes back to writing the shot.)

ASSISTANT WARDEN: *(Sotto voce)* God knows why the Warden let that teacher come in here. Meditating in prison. Anger management. What's next?

IDA: *(Peeking at the ASSISTANT WARDEN with one eye)* Yoga on the lawn? Ma'am?

ASSISTANT WARDEN: Was I talking to you?

IDA: No ma'am.

ASSISTANT WARDEN: Does it look like I need your advice?

IDA: No, ma'am.

ASSISTANT WARDEN: *(Staring at IDA)* I've got my eye on you, young lady. I know you're up to something and you can be sure I'm going to find out what it is. You can't fool me.

IDA: Yes, ma'am. *(Takes another deep breath and returns to meditating)*

ASSISTANT WARDEN: *(Checks her watch and finishes writing the shot.)* All right. You can go now.

(IDA meditatively walks towards stage right. ASSISTANT WARDEN watches her. IDA looks back as if to flip her the bird, but when she sees ASSISTANT WARDEN watching, she turns, resumes her meditative guise and keeps walking. ASSISTANT WARDEN exits stage left. IDA stops to address audience)

IDA: Goddamnit. Four shots in one week. That's a record even for me. Plus now she thinks I'm some crazy yogifying, meditating hippy. Like I need that shit on me too. *(Paces back and forth)* I don't understand what happens to me when I see her coming, or worse, that asshole Officer Peckerwood. All I know is I hate them. It's like my mind goes blank and something else takes over. I'm mad. Mad, mad mad. *(IDA clenches her fists)* Okay, Ida, get a grip. What would the teacher say? Oh yeah, what colors would you use if you painted how you feel inside? Red. It's all red. *(IDA clenches her eyes shut)* Screaming bloody red against black. Okay. Then what? Oh yeah, teacher would say what sensations are you feeling? I feel tight in my chest, like I can hardly get in enough air. Tight down my arms. Tight in my hands. Tight all over. Now what? Oh yeah, breathe into the feeling, let the feeling teach you something. Sure as hell hope teacher's right about this shit because here goes. *(Long beat as IDA gradually breathes faster, up in her chest)* I feel all clumsy and afraid, like when I was...like when I was fourteen and I come in the kitchen that one time...I'm late for school...Mama's yelling at me to hurry and that always messes me up and I spill the last of the milk...that sets the baby to crying...Papa comes in the back door all mean and blood-shot and smelling bad...he sees me....he grabs me...and next thing I know, I'm on the floor flat out...my eyes are swollen shut...my nose is bleeding... Baby's crying. Mama's screaming at me...she's saying it's all my fault...My fault! I look around to see if Papa's gone. Thank God he is. (With more intensity) But why didn't <u>she</u> do something? Why didn't she ever <u>do</u> something to keep him off of me!! Except to say it's all my fault...Sometimes, sometimes, I wish...I wish she was dead...I want to wrap my fingers around her throat...I want... I want to....

(IDA bends over and lets out a long belly scream. After a beat, OFFICER EDGEWOOD rushes in from stage right)

OFFICER EDGEWOOD: What in hell is going on here? Somebody attack you?

IDA: (Crouching on the ground) No. Go away.

OFFICER EDGEWOOD: Don't be telling me what to do, you little bitch. Sit up and look at me. (Approaches IDA)

IDA: Don't touch me. Don't come <u>near</u> me. <u>Don't touch me</u>! (IDA breaks into sobs)

OFFICER EDGEWOOD: *(Menacingly)* I'll do what I please and don't you forget it. *(Speaking into his radio)* Officer Edgewood requesting backup on the walkway. I repeat, Officer Edgewood requesting...

(ASSISTANT WARDEN rushes in from stage left)

ASSISTANT WARDEN: What's going on? Is she all right?

OFFICER EDGEWOOD: How should I know? I found her bent over screaming her head off. Freaking out. Resisting an officer.

ASSISTANT WARDEN: I'll take it from here.

OFFICER EDGEWOOD: But I've already put in the call...

ASSISTANT WARDEN: I've got it, Officer Edgewood. Thank you. You can go back to your duties.

OFFICER EDGEWOOD: *(After a long beat)* Whatever you say. Assistant Warden *(With contempt)* You the man.

(ASSISTANT WARDEN almost bites on this bait, but decides to let it go. OFFICER EDGEWOOD exits stage right)

ASSISTANT WARDEN: You okay Ida?

IDA: *(Blinking, pushing on her belly)* Yeah, I, I think so. Just feel kinda weird is all.

ASSISTANT WARDEN: *(Helps IDA straighten up)* I'm going to call the doctor.

IDA: Doctor? No, please don't. I'm okay. Really. Just a little lightheaded. Actually, I feel kinda good.

ASSISTANT WARDEN: You were bent over screaming and you say you feel good? Are you crazy?

IDA: No, not really. I guess I just had to let it out, that's all.

ASSISTANT WARDEN: Let what out?

IDA: I don't know. All I know is it was something old. Something deep.

ASSISTANT WARDEN: Uh huh. Well you like to give me a heart attack. Are you sure you're okay?

IDA: Yeah, I'm sure.

ASSISTANT WARDEN: Hey, this screaming isn't another thing you're learning in that stress group, is it?

IDA: No, ma'am. Well yeah. Sometimes. Maybe you should try it. You know, let it all out.

ASSISTANT WARDEN: Hey, don't push your luck. I've had just about enough of you today, young lady. Are you sure you're okay?

IDA: Yes ma'am, I feel really good.

ASSISTANT WARDEN: You're sufficiently recovered to make it back to your unit?

IDA: Yes ma'am.

ASSISTANT WARDEN: Without any more meditating or screaming?

IDA: Yes ma'am. *(Turns to go)*

ASSISTANT WARDEN: Wait just a minute Ida.

IDA: *(Stops in her tracks)* Uh oh.

ASSISTANT WARDEN: When I helped you up just now, I...I...well... I could tell you're not wearing a bra. That's against prison regulations. I'm going to have to give you another shot. And that makes five for the week, and that means a weekend in the SHU.

IDA: But Warden, please. You don't understand. There's something I got to tell you.

ASSISTANT WARDEN: *(Writing up the shot in her notebook)* What's that, young lady?

IDA: Well, see, the thing is Warden, I <u>am</u> wearing a bra. *(IDA pulls up her shirt just far enough to expose her stomach, around which is fastened a black bra. She ventures a very small grin)*

ASSISTANT WARDEN: *(With a stern look)* Young lady, you are trying my patience. You may be complying with the letter of the law, but certainly not the spirit. Do you really think that if you joke with me I'll forget to do my job?

IDA: No, not really.

ASSISTANT WARDEN: What was that?

IDA: No, I would never think that. Ma'am

ASSISTANT WARDEN: Good. Well, have you got anything else to say before you report to SHU?

IDA: Yes ma'am.

ASSISTANT WARDEN: I'm waiting.

IDA: Thanks for calling Officer Edgewood off me.

ASSISTANT WARDEN: *(Taken a little aback)* You're, uh, you're welcome. Anything else?

IDA: Good luck with your promotion.

ASSISTANT WARDEN: *(Very surprised)* Well, that's unexpected. Thank you. But don't think by flattering me you can weasel out of this.

IDA: No ma'am. *(Turning to go)* Well, I guess I'll find out if the SHU is a good place to meditate. 'Cause one thing's for sure.

ASSISTANT WARDEN: What's that?

IDA: I got plenty of time.

END

Soft Restraints

Author's Note: As mentioned in the note for *Something Old, Something Deep*, these two plays are inspired by my experience with the Prison Integrated Health Program between 1990 and 1994. One detail in *Soft Restraints* is the use of a hand-operated video camera to chronicle the suicide watch. A skeptical reader might ask why prison staff didn't use permanently mounted surveillance cameras. The answer in this particular case is that the room used for this suicide watch was not the regular one, and was therefore ill-equipped. But the question is important: in the long run, the growing trend towards privately-run prisons operating without public accountability or scrutiny ensures that contact between prison staff and prisoners is pared to a bare minimum, and permanently-mounted surveillance cameras are fast becoming ubiquitous.

Cast of Characters:

ALEESHA: an African-American prisoner, thin and bedraggled, wearing flip flops and dressed in an orange jumpsuit two sizes too big. Her wrists are cuffed in front with soft restraints, a kind of plastic handcuff. Her hair is braided in small tight braids.

OFFICER STILLS: a white female guard wearing heavy black shoes and dressed in a dark prison guard uniform a size too small. Clipped on her belt are a night stick, radio, and a large key ring. On her lapel is the microphone for the radio. She is operating a hand-held video camera.

TIME: Early 1990s

SETTING: A medical unit inside a women's prison. A small office at stage left, with a large window open to a hallway at stage right, has been pressed into service as a temporary suicide-watch room. Inside the room are a mattress and pillow on a single bed, and a wooden chair. The room is lit with an overhead fluorescent light.

AT RISE: ALEESHA paces from inside the locked suicide-watch room. In the hallway, OFFICER STILLS videotapes her through the window.

ALEESHA: *(Pressing her face and cuffed hands against the window, with low, bitter anger)* Get that thing outta my face. My lawyer's gonna hear 'bout this. Treatin' me this way. Like I was some animal in a goddamn zoo...Whatsa matter? You deaf or something? Can't you hear me through this window? I said, get that goddamn camera outta my face! Leave me alone.

OFFICER STILLS: Come on now. Prison regulations. Anyone on suicide watch has to be continually monitored for their own safety.

ALEESHA: Suicide-watch my ass. What, so you can watch me do it from behind a window? What kinda prison regulations is that shit?

OFFICER STILLS: Come on, Harmon. I've got to record every breath you take for the next 24 hours. Don't you know that by now?

ALEESHA: Well how come I ain't still in the SHU? How come I got dragged over here to the Medical Unit?

OFFICER STILLS: You get what you deserve. From what I heard, you made such a ruckus over there, they had to put you here so they can clean it up and let all the other prisoners settle down.

ALEESHA: Ruckus my ass. It was the damn guards that made the goddamn ruckus.

(ALEESHA stares into the camera. OFFICER STILLS keeps the video running. Garbled messages and loud static are heard over the radio on her lapel. ALEESHA turns her back and folds her arms in disgust)

You prison guards all alike. Just 'cause you a little woman like me don't make no difference. You're all mean. *(Turns toward OFFICER STILLS)* Did you hear me? You all mean and nasty. *(Turns away, paces the room, then presses back on the window, mocking)* Hey, Officer Mean and Nasty, hidin' behind yo' camera. Did you get how they manhandled me into this room? Did you get <u>that</u> all on tape?

(ALEESHA paces in a low fury. OFFICER STILLS keeps videotaping but with increasing discomfort)

It ain't right how they treat me. One fat guard feelin' me up. That other one pullin' on my leg. Those two blond bozos fightin' over which arm they're gonna twist. Dressed in all that riot gear. What are they so scared of? Bunch of keystone cops if you ask me. Like none of 'em knows how to pick up an itty bitty woman even when she's cuffed. *(Turning to the camera, preening her tight braids as best she can in the window's reflection)* But I gave 'em a good fight, didn't I? Surprised 'em. I may be small, but I'm strong...Did you get all that? I sure hope so. 'Cause when my lawyer gets a hold of that tape and sees how those racist mothers treated me, he gonna sue your asses. Cruel and unusual punishment, for sure. *(ALEESHA starts pacing again)*. Nobody has to go to some third world country. They're doin' it to us right here in Uncle Sam. Treating me like I was some terrorist murderin' bitch...Shit. They oughtta meet my cell-mate.

OFFICER STILLS: (Turning the radio switch on her lapel, OFFICER STILLS listens to a garbled voice full of loud and crackling static) Officer Stills here on suicide watch...What's that? ...You're breaking up...Oh, yeah, Edgewood, no problem...(Lowering her voice) It's Harmon. No, looks like she'll settle down soon...Yeah, another feisty one.

(ALEESHA, who is listening, turns in disgust with her hands in fists. OFFICER STILLS notices, lowers her voice again)

What's that?...She was in the SHU and smashed the overhead light...Yeah, glass everywhere...No I don't know why... (ALEESHA presses her ear against the window) What?... You're taking bets?

ALEESHA: (To herself) That's low.

OFFICER STILLS: (To the radio) Jeez, Edgewood, you guys are cold... Oh, oh, I thought you meant taking bets on when she'd, you know... Oh, you mean like when she'll get quiet. Well, in that case I guess I'm in. Put me down for...(Looks at ALEEHSA and then at her watch)... another three hours. Yeah, 10 pm...Yeah, five bucks....

ALEESHA: (Walks over to the bed, sits, hugs pillow to her stomach) Where do they find you people?

OFFICER STILLS: *(To the radio)* No, that's all I can afford... Look, Edgewood, mind your own business, OK?... No, I am not going out with you Friday...I said no... And would you please quit calling me baby? *(looking at ALEESHA to make sure she can't hear)* Harmon's file?... No, I didn't...She did what?...With a cleaver?...Jesus... Both of them?...A year ago today?...You better not be bullshitting me...Right....OK.

ALEESHA: *(Rocking herself, with increasing intensity)* What am I gonna do? How am I gonna get through this? It ain't even worth it. Oh my babies, my twins, my babies... *(Begins to wail)*

OFFICER STILLS: *(To the radio)* Gotta go....Right. Over and out. *(Switches radio off. Stiffly)* Hey, Harmon, that's enough. Settle down.

ALEESHA: *(Catches herself, sits up, wipes tears away. Mockingly)* You still got that camera on? Did you get how that fat guard jumped back when I spit on him? Like I got AIDS or somethin'. He look like he wanna go cry to his mama. Serve him right, putting these goddamned handcuffs on me. Soft restraints my ass. *(Facing OFFICER STILLS at the window, holding her cuffed hands up)* Hey! Can't you do nothin' about these cuffs? They're too tight!... What's the matter? You the flunkie? Got no say-so? *(Turning away, looking with more interest at the objects in the room)* Shit, I hate women who ain't got no self-respect. Nothin' worse than a woman who got some power but ain't got the balls to use it.

(OFFICER STILLS adjusts the camera, presses at her low back. ALEESHA keeps ranting with increasing anger throughout)

Reminds me of my pity-ass sister, goddamn her, leavin' me with that asshole. And smokin' all my crack. Why she have to give me up like that? That shit ain't right. Nothin' worse than a goddamn snitch. It ain't fair. She's free. And I gotta do twenty to life.

(In a burst of rage and frustration, ALEESHA screams. She grabs the pillow and slams it against the chair and the bed, breaking the pillow open. OFFICER STILLS speaks nervously into the lapel microphone. We hear loud static)

(Overlapping)

OFFICER STILLS: Officer Stills here on suicide watch.

ALEESHA: *(Taking off her flip flops, jumping up on the chair)* It ain't right. It ain't fair. Goddamn snitchin' bitch.

OFFICER STILLS: I need backup ASAP. Ah, prisoner out of control... Broken glass possible....Please advise...

ALEESHA: *(From atop the chair, ALEESHA tries to smash the overhead light with her flip flops, but can't quite reach it)* Soon as I get out I'm gonna kill your sorry ass. Betray me like. Accuse me of murder.

ALEESHA: *(With intense frustration)* My own sister. Stabbing me in the back. Hope you rot in hell. Goddamn you. I'll show you. *(ALEESHA tries once more to smash the overhead light, then throws her flip-flops against the wall. She jumps on the bed, slams her body against the wall, cries and screams, then upends the bed in a rage and jumps up on the chair)*

OFFICER STILLS: *(Urgently into the radio)* Advise, I repeat, please advise...Over? *(Beat. To herself)* Shit. Edgewood you bastard. *(Remembers the camera, adjusts it to aim at ALEESHA. Takes a deep breath. To ALEESHA, stiffly)* Look what you did. You shouldn't behave like that. You're only making it worse on yourself.

(ALEESHA roars. OFFICER STILLS fumbles with the switch on her microphone. With more authority)

Officer Stills here on suicide watch in the Medical Unit. Prisoner out of control, in possible danger. Broken glass a possibility, I repeat, broken glass. Request immediate backup. Please advise. Do you copy? Over. *(Again, static on the radio. OFFICER STILLS grimaces)* Goddamn them.

(OFFICER STILLS shuts off the microphone. ALEESHA starts to step down off the chair)

Whoa, wait up there Harmon. You don't want to be walking on that floor.

ALEESHA: *(Still overwrought)* Why the hell not?

OFFICER STILLS: Because there might be broken glass on the floor.

ALEESHA: Shut up and leave me alone. What do you care?

OFFICER STILLS: You could cut your feet. You don't want to hurt yourself.

ALEESHA: How the hell would you know what I want? Besides, there ain't no broken glass in here. Not on the floor anyway. *(Carefully picks a shard of glass she has hidden in her braids and makes sure OFFICER STILLS can see it)* Where's your camera now? Why don't you tape this? *(Makes a slow, deliberate slashing movement with the shard. Studies OFFICER STILLS)* You could put it all on video. I could cut myself real good and you could play it for the goon squad on your day off. Get a good laugh. Win your bet. Watch some skinny black bitch bleed to death right in front your eyes. *(Maneuvers her hands in the soft restraints so the shard is positioned over her wrist)*

OFFICER STILLS: Whoa, wait a minute. Don't do that. Come on now. Put the glass down.

ALEESHA: Why should I?

OFFICER STILLS: Look. I'm not like those other guards. I wouldn't want to see you cut yourself. Come on now, don't do anything you'll regret.

ALEESHA: (Mockingly) Hah, that's rich. Don't do nothin' I'll regret. Child, I already done that. How you suppose I got to prison in the first place?

(Beat. They stare at each other)

OFFICER STILLS: Yeah, well, you got a point there.

ALEESHA: (Looking down at the shard of glass in her hand) I sure as hell do.

OFFICER STILLS: (Beat. Softly) Come on, help me out here. You're in a fix, no doubt about that. I don't want you to get hurt. Put the glass down. Please.

ALEESHA: Yeah, if I get hurt, your ass'll be in trouble. That's how it is, ain't it, (Mockingly) Officer low man on the totem pole?

OFFICER STILLS: (Reluctantly) Yeah, that's how it works. You don't really want to hurt yourself, do you? Come on... Hey, I don't even know your name.

ALEESHA: (Standing back on the chair) Yes, you do.

OFFICER STILLS: No, I mean your first name.

ALEESHA: Oh, so now we gonna be friends? My road dog, is that it?

OFFICER STILLS: Look. You going to help me out or not?

ALEESHA: You don't need my help. You the one with the radio and the camera and the goon squad.

OFFICER STILLS: Look, we won't even need backup if you cooperate.

ALEESHA: You ain't gonna call those big bastards so they can manhandle me?

OFFICER STILLS: No. Not unless you give me trouble.

ALEESHA: 'Cause I won't stand for it. I'll put up a big fight. I'll cut them if they hurt me. I'll cut my own self. *(Turning toward OFFICER STILLS)* How are you any different? Why should I trust you?

OFFICER STILLS: Because I'm a woman. You can trust me. Woman to woman.

ALEESHA: Where have I hear that shit before? Look, sister, it was another woman that put me in this joint.

OFFICER STILLS: But I'm not her.

ALEESHA: Then who the hell are you?

OFFICER STILLS: (Squirming) I'm, I'm...(Puts camera down, looks
at it for a long beat, then approaches the window) Look, I'm
not supposed to....It's against regulations to talk...Oh
crap. Look, I know what it's like to get manhandled.
I know what it's like to...to stare at the wallpaper,
memorize every flower, because, because...Look, let's
just say I know all about it. And I never want that
to happen again...Not to me, not to you, not to any
woman. That's why I became a prison guard, so no
one would mess with me...so no one would... (OFFICER
STILLS catches herself) That's all.

(A long beat as the women take each other's measure. ALEESHA
squats back down on the chair)

ALEESHA: (Holding shard away from her) I think I know what
you're talkin' about.

OFFICER STILLS: I just think there's a better way. An easier
way. Just you and me. But it'll only work if you promise
to help me.

ALEESHA: What kinda help are you talkin' about?

OFFICER STILLS: I need you to sit down on that chair and hold your feet off the floor. Can you do that for me?

ALEESHA: But I already told you, ain't no broken glass on the floor. Only here, in my hand.

OFFICER STILLS: I see it. We're coming to that. But for right now, I'm going to come inside, nice and slow. You're going to stay on that chair? You're going to stay cool?

ALEESHA: Yeah, I'm cool.

(OFFICER STILLS *unlocks the door and enters. Another pause while they size each other up. OFFICER STILLS looks for glass on the floor. Seeing none, she retrieves ALEESHA'S flip flops, hands them to her, rights the bed and sits on it. ALEESHA puts on flip flops, relaxes her feet*)

ALEESHA: Told you there wasn't any glass on the floor.

OFFICER STILLS: I had to be sure.

ALEESHA: OK. So now what?

OFFICER STILLS: I'm working on it. *(Long beat)* Look, I want to keep helping you, but I need you to cooperate.

ALEESHA: *(With a slight edge)* I been cooperatin'.

OFFICER STILLS: Yeah, you have. But we're not out of the woods yet.

ALEESHA: So what you plannin' on doin'?

OFFICER STILLS: I'm going take you back to your room in the SHU. But before I move you, I've got to call for backup. *(ALEESHA goes rigid)* Prison regulations. *(ALEESHA shakes her head)* Look, those big guys aren't going to touch you as long as you stick with me. I promise. But I need your word on that.

ALEESHA: Why should I believe you?

OFFICER STILLS: Because you've got to believe somebody, and I'm all you got right now.

ALEESHA: *(Raising her hand-cuffed hands)* What about these?

OFFICER STILLS: You know I can't take them off, but I can see about loosening them. What about that?

(OFFICER STILLS gestures toward the shard in ALEESHA'S hand. Long tense beat. ALEESHA palms the shard, then puts her hands out. Another tense beat)

You sure you want to play it this way?

(ALEESHA nods. Beat)

Okay then, cuffs first.

(*OFFICER STILLS loosens the cuffs warily. ALEESHA stands rock still*)

Damn things get tighter the more you struggle. There, better?

(*ALEESHA nods*)

Now, your turn.

(*Long pause before ALEESHA drops the shard to the floor. OFFICER STILLS carefully picks it up and puts it in the breast pocket of her uniform*)

Thank you. Ready?

ALEESHA: No, not yet. There's something else. I want to know your full name.

OFFICER STILLS: You know we can't be friends.

ALEESHA: Shit, you think I'm some crazy fool?

OFFICER STILLS: No, I don't. I can think of <u>some</u> people around here who <u>are</u> crazy, but you're not one of them. My name's June. June Olivia Stills.

ALEESHA: June. I'm Aleesha. Aleesha Rose Harmon.

(They shake awkwardly)

Gotta tell you something else, June.

OFFICER STILLS: What's that, Aleesha?

ALEESHA: You best find yourself another job, girl. You ain't
       mean enough to be no prison guard.

*(OFFICER STILLS nods and smiles a little. They rise. OFFICER
STILLS calls for backup. We hear very loud static again. OFFICER
STILLS shakes her head and turns off the microphone, then takes
ALEESHA gently by the elbow and both exit. The camera is long
forgotten)*

END

ACKNOWLEDGEMENTS

To just a few of my many teachers: Richard and Maud Green Park, Gordon Newell, David Park, Robert Walker, Aaron Abeyta, Carol Guerrero-Murphy, Rachel Manley, Jane Brox, Kate Snodgrass and my horse, Esperanza—thank you for the daily inspiration of living your lives with fortitude, conviction, and honesty.

To my editor and publisher: Stewart Warren of Mercury HeartLink—thank you for midwifing this entire process, for pressing me to tell the truth and for reminding me to carve my writing. Some pieces truly do work better when I "ditch the last paragraph."

To my readers: Kate Booth, Trudi Kretzinger, Judy Burrell, Peter Weiss, Frances Vander Stappen, Candelora Versace and Cynthia Green—thank you all for your sharp eyes, cogent suggestions, and gyroscopic sense of when the work was off balance or missing something.

To the catalyst for this project: Dr. David MacWilliams—that you for suggesting that my application for assistant professor of creative writing would gain gravitas if I published a new work of fiction. Whether I get that position or not, this work may well have languished inside the digital viscera of my laptop had you not dropped that bomb on me.

To my soulmate: Henry Woolbert—thank you, always and forever, for having my back and being my buddy on this wild ride.

www.ingramcontent.com/pod-product-compliance
Lightning Source LLC
Chambersburg PA
CBHW020654260626
47157CB00008B/3025